"*Hidden Shadow* is an engaging tale of secrets, ghosts, unexpected romance, and searching for the place you belong. The prohibition era mystery will draw you in but it's Sophie and her cast of friends and found family who keep you reading."
—Celia Mulder

"A clever work of art about hidden family secrets and what fate has to offer. Jennifer Bourland will leave you desperately wanting to learn more. You won't sleep until you've reached the last page."
—Maria Graessle

"This book had me hooked from the first chapter. *Hidden Shadow* is suspenseful and romantic. It will keep you guessing until the very end. Jennifer Bourland is an exquisite writer."
—Tami Ford

"A thrilling journey through Sophie's life, finding a new place she was destined for. Filled with mystery and a beautiful romance, *Hidden Shadow* is a page turner from the beginning all the way to the end."
—Meredith Voakes

"Feel yourself falling back in time as you immerse yourself reading this beautiful mystery."
—Dr. Rachal Mittleman

© 2022 Jennifer Bourland

ISBN: 978-1-63988-642-5
Library of Congress Control Number: 2022918997

Published by Atmosphere Press

Cover design by Matthew Fielder

atmospherepress.com

PROLOGUE

"The mind is its own place, and in itself can make
a Heaven of Hell, a Hell of Heaven."
   —*John Milton*

Macie Brooks could see the familiar neon sign of the Blue Owl illuminated at the end of the block. The brisk walk there tonight was different. Revenge consumed her thoughts. She ignored the bite of the January late-night air, which created rapid puffs of visible and whiskey-scented breath in front of her as her movement increased. The material of her long black cloak swayed from side to side, brushing against her lanky calves. To her left, Macie heard a low rumble of a vehicle. Keeping her head down, she hoped it was not a police car making its nightly pass through, looking for any excuse to search patrons or establishments suspected of alcohol possession or consumption. The 1929 Lincoln, slowly rumbling along the paved downtown road of the Motor City, provided momentary relief.

Tensions were already heightened and causing sleepless nights in this era of rum-running and backroom speakeasies. After word that the authorities were ramping up and conducting even more searches of local establishments, they were worried that relying on a secret password wouldn't provide the added security speakeasy owners needed. There was a growing interest with unfamiliar people attending. Informants were on the rise, which became the source of many of the raids, leaving it difficult to recognize who was trustworthy. Macie and her two partners had taken precautions to close the Indigo Room, an underground speakeasy in the cellar of the Blue Owl. They hoped it would be just for a few days until the threat of pursuits against local business owners settled down. Closure of the room and temporary halt of alcohol sales would bring a shortage of anticipated cash, but even more unsettling was the fear that the hidden contraband would be discovered, and they would be exposed.

A new enemy emerged. One beyond the authorities, beyond the financial distress. An enemy within. Recent events caused suspicions of betrayal by the partners and friends she trusted for many years. A few nights ago, she overheard part of a conversation between her other two business partners. Since hearing her name mentioned, along with the topic of conversation, her mind was cluttered with uneasiness. Macie knew she could not approach or confront them, leaving her more isolated now than ever. The stress was invading her sleep at night and consuming her thoughts by day. The shock and emotional pain were equally competing for space. It was almost as if she were just a vessel of numbness to anything other than frustration and betrayal. The three of them had a thriving partnership in business for so long. Now it was that very group she could not trust. She wondered where it went wrong. Anger rising inside her, she had to do something about it. Those in her immediate circle had to pay for the deceit and the betrayal.

The intent was to get in and out without being noticed or at least without engaging too much to be suspected of anything other than her normal routine. As she approached the building, there were a few people coming out of the door. They were distracted by their own conversation and laughter, but gave a quick nod and smile to Macie, long enough to hold the door. Music and conversation were becoming louder as she made her way inside. She slipped through the middle of the room, weaving through a few small groups of people. Macie knew the door to the cellar would be locked, and the skeleton key that opened it, along with the other rooms underground, was in the desk drawer in the office. She turned the corner and entered the doorway to the office. Focused on her mission, she almost didn't see the little girl sitting in the chair behind the desk, looking up at her with a quiet smile. A strand of her chin-length, dark brown hair fell from behind her ear, brushing the side of her face when she held up her stuffed lion. Its translucent, marbled green eyes matched the girl's. She waved at Macie with the small, plush lion's paw. Macie returned the quiet smile and continued toward the desk drawer. She was slightly surprised to see the owner's seven-year-old daughter, Hazel, there so late. It was not uncommon to see her make an appearance during the day, sitting in the office from time to time, occupying herself while her mother stopped in or worked for a short time.

A sudden uneasiness came over Macie. She only had a few seconds to commit to a decision. She could turn back and forget the whole thing. The constant collision between opposing forces in her mind was exhausting. They had to pay, she reminded herself. Anger and frustration resurfacing. Something had to be done, tonight.

After grabbing the key, she quickly turned and left the office without a word or another glance at the girl, afraid anything other than a swift exit would influence her decision. She looked around cautiously but casually, making sure no one saw her approaching the door to the cellar. It was a massive solid wood door with a unique-looking lock that took an intricate skeleton key to pass through it. Cautiously scanning the area again, she unlocked the curved door with metal trim. Tucking the key away in her pocket, she clicked the switch that turned on the light to illuminate the dark staircase leading down to the cellar. As she pulled the door behind her, the weight left it open a crack. Macie slowly climbed down to the bottom, looking up at the top of the stairway to make sure she was alone. The dim light made it difficult to see. She found the chain for the light at the bottom of the stairway and pulled it on, exposing a long hallway perpendicular to the stairway. A storage room at the end of the hall on the left was closer than what they called the Indigo Room at the opposite end of the hall on the right. Each door similar to the cellar stairway door. Large, solid, dark wood with black metal hinges and a curve at the top. She headed to the storage room where all the inventory of liquor was kept. Looking back over her shoulder, she had to make sure nobody was coming up behind her. It wouldn't be out of the ordinary for her to be down there as one of the owners; it was a daily occurrence. The plan tonight was to get in and out without being noticed.

Unlocking a similar door with the same key, she walked into the storage room, found the light, and pulled the string. This one had a shorter string and was difficult to pull on. Squinting slightly from the dull glow of light, she glanced around the storage room lined with wooden shelves. It was old but built sturdy to hold all the bottles of illegal substances sold under the radar along with a few whiskey barrels. She grabbed a new bottle of gin off the shelf, opened it, and took a sip to calm her nerves. It didn't push out the pain and the anger. Surfacing with a vengeance as the memory replayed, she made one last attempt with a long pull on the bottle. Then she sailed it across the room. Clear liquid and glass violently crashed against the wall. She picked up a wooden stick, just smaller than a baseball bat, laying on one of the shelves. Tears fell down her face while she struck the bottles on the shelves, knocking them into each other and crashing to the floor. She worked quickly in case the noise was heard above, unlikely though since the music would deafen the sound. She stepped through the puddles of liquid and shards of glass all over the floor, crunching beneath her feet. The sharp smell of alcohol was potent in the small space. She dropped the stick on the ground, pulled off the light, and locked the door behind her, not realizing she had been seen.

The battle in the mind can be the worst, most complicated battle of all. Chaos inside contradicting what others see is peaceful, calm. All the troubles and complications of her life appeared much simpler before that night, but Macie didn't know it then. She was completely unaware that she would become part of a secret that would be hidden for generations to come. What she wouldn't give to go back. It was too late and the peace of mind she had at one time was gone. She looked around and saw more darkness than light.

The legend of the hauntings and the unexplained events were documented by few but spoken by many. According to the legend, as guests walked through the cellar hallway to the Indigo Room, one of the city's known speakeasies, her spirit haunted the hallway. Whispers, cries, and mysterious noises have been heard on many occasions and strange occurrences have taken place over many years. Fear of the unknown has deterred some guests from entering. For others, it has become an attraction and has drawn them in. Some locals reported hearing a child's cry in the cellar of The Blue Owl.

CHAPTER 1

PRESENT DAY

Reed Manor was buzzing with energy from the hustle and bustle of the catering and housekeeping staff preparing for the surprise event of the year. Sophie Thomas, psychologist, and occasional dabbler in interior design, was finalizing a project she had been working on for the past couple of months. Her client, Harlan Reed, spared no expense for his wife's 60th birthday party. He wanted a classy, intimate (of which he considered 80 of their closest family and friends) dinner party, with an authentic "Roaring Twenties" theme. This being her first project for him and a referral by a mutual friend, she hoped everything was satisfactory. He was very particular and loved history, including stories of the past, culture, anything dealing with people. He had many connections to influential people. Everything Harlan did was always over the top and so were his expectations. This project was a massive undertaking, more than just decorating for a birthday celebration. It required lavish renovations to his home in order for his wife and their guests to be able to imagine the experience of stepping back in time. His vision was to transform his home through the décor, the music, the food, and the fashion from almost 100 years ago. There was also the time constraint to contend with. Grayce Reed was vacationing with friends at their second home in Louisiana for two months. Harlan thought it would provide a perfect opportunity to orchestrate his wish. He was confident that Sophie could help him make this happen. She did not want to disappoint. Her reputation and her clients were on the line.

The creative challenge of working on this project, a cross between design and event coordinating, was a refreshing change of pace from diagnosing disorders of various types and following up with treatment objectives. It was a creative distraction that she occasionally took on, mostly for family and friends. A distant career from her past that she never fully left. She engaged herself in work, giving attention to the two projects she was designing for two different clients. Sophie had some extra time for a few more weeks to take on the two projects. At least until her new job with a busy, full-time case load started. She was offered a position as a clinical psychologist at a small practice not far from her apartment near the suburbs. The projects would be completed just in time for her new job to start. Things were working out smoothly.

Harlan was a hands-on kind of guy. Since he had most of the research covered, she focused more on the overall layout and tracking down other antiques, something she never thought she would enjoy so much. Sophie found that particular time period fascinating, charmed by the music, fashion, and antiques. It was an interest she shared with her client and his wife Grayce.

The Reeds both grew up in Detroit and now live in a gorgeous, 8,000-square-foot home in the desirable suburb of Lake Pointe, Michigan. Their modern architecture-style home already had a neutral décor as a base, providing the perfect canvas to add furniture pieces, accessories, and wall art. Harlan and his wife have always admired Art Deco and have been fascinated with the architecture of the Detroit skyline, which Sophie incorporated into the design. Its clean lines, angles, geometric shapes, and metallic gold added to the authenticity.

Harlan provided a wealth of historical knowledge, especially relating to this particular time period, almost like he found out his wife was interested in it and learned everything he could about it. He also had the charm of being an excellent storyteller, captivating his audience, a quality which Sophie admired. In her experience, she was more of a listener. Education and career training in psychology only polished her natural abilities.

As a liquor enthusiast, Harlan was ecstatic to share all about how Detroit, Chicago, and New York were big cities for speakeasies during Prohibition. Detroit, being so close to Canada, was a popular port. The dangerous yet exhilarating missions of the rum runners smuggling alcohol between Canada and Detroit fascinated him. Harlan enjoyed the thrill of establishments with secret rooms and code words, all while staying under the radar of both ends of the spectrum, avoiding law enforcement and mobsters. He had the knowledge, and Sophie had the creativity to make his vision a success. They were both eagerly anticipating the event in which they could all, especially his wife Grayce, harvest the fruits of their labor.

Sweeping through the home one last time, straightening and making sure everything was in place, Sophie noticed her favorite piece from the project. It was a vintage, oil-rubbed, bronze rotary telephone. The base was covered with intricate, embossed curved lines. The handset wore a contrasting, crosshatch pattern and rested delicately on the base in perfect balance. It was resting on a sofa table among other accessories and furniture pieces in the great room. The home had an expansive openness that was perfect for entertaining. The marble flooring from the entry flowed through the great room and dining room, delivering a seamless look.

The charm and sophistication of the fashion worn by the arriving guests offered a genuine aspect to the costumes that heightened the excitement of the event. The women were in beautiful silk and satin evening wear. The length of the sleek, delicate gloves accented the flared, sweeping hem of the gowns. Men were dressed in dashing suits with coordinating Fedoras and Newsboy hats. Guests entered the grand foyer that had symmetrically placed, elegant, curved staircases. The red carpet for the guests was a striking contrast against the ivory-colored marble flooring. Above them, a contemporary, crystal pendant ceiling chandelier caught the attention of several guests as it sparkled from the reflection of the lighting.

Shortly after all the guests were accounted for, news came in that the lady of the house arrived and was about to make her grand entrance. Knowing how surprises can go either way, Sophie was hoping that Grayce would enjoy the care that her husband put into this evening. She was curious if her boyfriend Logan would ever go to those extremes down the road after they have been married. Nothing yet for wedding plans of her own, but with the possibility of moving in together in the next few days, things were moving in that direction.

Conversations regarding admiration of the atmosphere and the costumes quickly turned to whispers, then silence as the crowd took their places, filling in any inconspicuous areas behind the staircases. A shadow appeared behind the colorful stained-glass window flanking the length of the front door. Anticipation grew every second. The click of the lock on the door overtook the silence in the room. As the door pushed open, all eyes were looking for that moment of realization that the intruder was the unsuspecting guest of honor. The crowd was prepared and waiting for that precise moment to play their part. "Surprise!" the guests roared in unison. Grayce covered her mouth in delight and shock at the same time as emotion filled her face. Her wide eyes welled up. The crowd swarmed around her, swallowing her up with birthday greetings.

When she got her bearings, her husband gently welcomed her. They exchanged a sweet, intimate greeting, smiling at each other. He presented her with a stunning red satin floor-length gown, long, elegant silver gloves, and heels to match. She was impressed with the understated fitted style that offset the bold color. The cutout in back gave the dress an alluring effect. She was thrilled to wear it and amazed that this was all for her. Harlan, a devoted husband, adored his wife as much as she adored him. Even though they may have had their share of problems as many other couples, they were not only still together after 40 years, but truly happy.

Grayce politely parted from her company for a short time to dress for the occasion. The festivities were underway as the band filled the room with jazz, blues, and swing music. Guests were enjoying the food, drinks, and fashion, admiring costumes. When she returned, Grayce had transformed from travel clothes into an elegantly dressed woman. The gown looked even more amazing on her, fitting the shape of her slight curves perfectly. Her dark hair, all one length, stopped just above the shoulders. She had the type of thick, naturally wavy hair that without much effort could appear both elegant and casual. Her face, with its true simple beauty, gave her sixty years a youthful look. Harlan's expectations had been exceeded when he saw his wife return looking just as beautiful as the day he married her. As he took her hand, he leaned in, kissed her cheek, and mentioned how extraordinary she was. He guided his wife over to Sophie for an introduction. Sophie was enchanted by their approach and admired the love they shared even after so many years together. She hoped to be as happy in her own relationship.

"Grayce, I'd like you to meet Sophie Thomas. She is the one with the vision and creativity that made this idea come to life," Harlan said.

The three of them walked around as Harlan pointed out strategically placed accessories. These details that his wife hadn't seen yet included an antique telephone, vintage typewriter, and the cubism-inspired artwork hanging on the walls. Grayce admired the vintage furniture pieces placed throughout the home. She looked around with an exceptionally large approving smile on her face, amazed at the transformation of her home and the authenticity of the pieces.

"Thank you, Sophie. Thank you so much for doing all of this and all your hard work, love. It's such a wonderful surprise. I never, in a million years, would have expected all this." Grayce's eyes were welling up with tears again. "It must have been so much work. I can't get over how much detail went into all this. Everything is so beautiful."

Grayce Reed was the type of woman that people took an instant liking to. She was sincere. There was nothing superficial about the way she treated others, despite her social status. She was very appreciative of what she had and was very generous with her time and money. Her education was evident in her conversation. Most importantly, so was her sense of others. She always knew the right questions to ask. With many endearing qualities, Sophie had an immediate connection to her like they had been family her entire life. This familiarity was rare and comforting since Sophie was distant from her own family. As an only child from a small family with no traditions or genealogical interest, that's just the way it had always been. After a few minutes, Harlan was called away by a guest. Grayce and Sophie continued the conversation in his absence.

"Harlan tells me that you have always been fascinated with this era," Sophie said.

"Yes, it's a very intriguing time period. I much prefer the modern conveniences, but the music, fashion, and the photography have always been of interest to me," Grayce said.

The two women walked toward a collection of old photos hanging on the wall. "I love the black and white photography, and there is something unique about the expressions and the appearance compared to modern photos," Sophie said.

Gently holding on to Sophie's arm Grayce said, "You know, love, what really piqued my interest was a dream I had several years back. I can still remember so vividly. It was almost as if I was transported back to that time. It was bright and colorful, and I could hear the sound of the old cars and smell the food coming from the restaurants as I walked down the sidewalk downtown. The sweet smell of fresh pastries from a bakery. There was such a feeling of peace in that moment. That's all I remember, but it felt like more than just a dream, like a real memory. Ever since then, I have been intrigued by anything relating to that time." She smiled. "Have you had dreams like that before? Where they seem so real?" Grayce asked.

If Grayce only knew how true that was and how one dream in particular continued to haunt Sophie. Hesitatingly, but unusually comfortable enough to finally share with someone, to speak the words out loud, Sophie said, "Actually, yes." She paused. "I do have vivid dreams and recently had one more haunting than pleasant like the one you had."

The conversation was interrupted by a cackle of laughter from three ladies, elegantly dressed in navy blue. They were friends of the guest of honor. They had been waiting patiently for time with Grayce and reached their limit. After a couple of drinks, they were less concerned about the intrusion and more concerned with reminiscing. Hearing the words "Remember that time when…" was Sophie's cue to break away. Sophie enjoyed talking with Grayce but was surprisingly relieved by the interruption. She was thankful she didn't reveal anything more about her own dream to someone she just met. "Grayce, it was so nice to meet you, and I'm so glad I could help make it a memorable birthday for you," Sophie said.

"It was such a pleasure to meet you too, love. Thank you again for all your efforts. The transformation is truly incredible." Embracing her in a genuine hug. "It really is exceptional," Grayce said.

As Sophie stepped away, the group of ladies filled her spot, engulfing Grayce in conversation and recalling memorable stories from their past. Grayce was fully aware that Sophie had much more to say about her dream from the disquiet in her eyes, but she knew it wasn't the time to inquire. She was confident another opportunity would present itself or she would create one.

Sophie's job here was done, so she found an appropriate time to make her exit after a quick goodbye to Harlan. She made her way across the great room to find him near the cocktails. Thoughts of relief were running through her mind that she did not give Grayce details about her dream, especially not knowing what emotions would be stirred up. After all, she had just met the woman, and it was a joyous occasion.

When Sophie approached, Harlan was engaged in conversation with a few other friends. They were all intently listening to him. She smiled; being familiar with the story he was telling. She was amused as to what was coming as she saw the object he was holding in his hand. "They couldn't be too careful. Several had secret codes to get in. The Blue Owl had a speakeasy in the dark, dingy cellar called the Indigo Room. When you reached the door, only the ones who knew the correct code phrase could get in. You had to say, 'Uncle Charley is coming to town.' If they responded with 'he's bringing his dog too,' the room was open for business. If they responded with 'hope he is not bringing his dog,' that meant closed for business, in fear of authorities closing in," Harlan said.

A couple more guests had joined the group. Harlan looked up at the two ladies, including them in his next story. "Ladies, I know you both have extensive shoe collections, after many shopping trips with Grayce. I bet you've never seen this kind of shoe." Harlan held up a wooden block with areas carved out. "It's a Cow Shoe. Moonshiners would strap this on their feet. You think heels are uncomfortable. This would disguise any footprints left behind so they would look like they were from a cow," Harlan explained. "The steaks were high. They had to steer clear of trouble, udderwise there would be some real danger."

"We're very moo-ved by your story, Harlan," one of the guests responded playfully.

Sophie was hanging back near the end of a lineup of barstools, listening to the cheesy but mildly amusing banter. The bartender asked if Sophie could keep an eye out for a minute while he went to get more wine. She obliged and a guest happened to walk up seconds later.

"What can I get you?" Sophie asked, positioning herself behind the serving area.

"Hmm, I can't decide. Suggestions?" asked the woman with a curly blond wig and silver sequins sparkling on her headband.

Sophie paused for a second, scanning the variety of liquor bottles on deck, rested and ready for action. "I have just the thing if you like gin."

"I'm game."

Sophie mixed gin, honey and squeezed juice from a lemon and added another for garnish.

"Here ya go. Let me know what you think. It's one of my favorites," Sophie said.

The lady held up her glass, nodding a cheers to Sophie and took a small sip from the glass. "Delish! Thank you. What do you call this?"

"Bee's Knees," Sophie said.

"Thanks again." The woman smiled as she turned and headed toward the appetizers, the layers of fringe on her white flapper dress swaying as she shifted slightly out of the way of the bartender returning to his post with a crate of wine bottles in his arms.

The sounds of reactions after his story broke the intensity and gave Sophie a chance to interject a quick goodbye to Harlan. He asked her to stay and have a couple drinks, holding his glass up toward her, but she mentioned that she had to finish some packing for her move to her new apartment in a few days. He thanked her again for making the evening exactly what he had envisioned. He assured her that he was in her debt.

The ambient glow of the house filled with warmth and celebration disappeared from sight as she stepped outside and closed the door behind her. The lively music and conversation faded as she gained distance from the house, making her way down the car-lined driveway. It was suddenly quiet, too quiet, and her light jacket wasn't enough to keep the chill off her skin. The September moon was out and illuminated an otherwise dark sky. A light wind turned into a sudden gust, blowing her hair and flapping the bottom of her dress in its wake. She had a thought to turn around and go back inside the house. She didn't realize how comforting it was to have been in there until the moment she closed the door.

In an attempt to escape the elements, she trotted in her heels the rest of the way to her car, while carefully focusing on not stumbling. Entering her car was a reprieve from the wind, but not from the creeping thoughts of her recurring dream she started to tell Grayce about. She closed her eyes in an attempt to avoid dredging up the details. She had that knot in the pit of her stomach, that cold twinge of anxiousness rising from her mid-section to her head, through her arms and legs like an intruder running through her veins. Then she gave in to the memory of the dream.

A long, narrow street in New Orleans was filled with people celebrating Mardi Gras. There were flashes of close-up faces full of smiles and laughter, like viewing them from the other side of a camera. The parade of people turned a corner. She was lagging behind after dropping something. She looked up to see the tail end of the crowd leaving the street vacant. It was almost silent as the noise dissolved. The sound of footsteps from behind caught her attention. She turned to see a tall, dark figure. At a closer glance, it appeared to be a person dressed in a long cloak with a hood covering its head. They started walking toward her slowly at first then picking up the pace. Paralyzed by fear, she froze for a second. Her flight response kicked in as she walked briskly down the middle of the street. The walk immediately turned into a run as she turned her head back and saw the rapidly closing distance behind her and the flowing material at the bottom of the cloak. It was just behind her now. A large wooden door was in sight just a few steps away. She headed toward it, hoping she could get on the other side of it, separating her from the assailant. The footsteps behind her were audible now on the pavement beneath her. She couldn't look back. She wouldn't. Just keep focused on the door. The lock. *Is it open? I hope it's open. It better be!*

She had one shot. In her attempt to reach the door, she took a larger leap forward. Her foot slipped on the confetti-dusted pavement. Losing her balance, she slammed into the thick wood door and thumped to the ground. Half conscious, she struggled to open her eyes, feeling the jarring pain all over her body. It was difficult to hear. The picture was hazy, fading in toward the edges, like watching a movie with a light flickering on and off. She wanted to focus until it became clear that a figure with a skeleton mask was standing over her. The figure slowly reached up to remove the mask and the face of an older woman was revealed. The image came into focus more as the mysterious woman leaned in closer. Her face became larger every inch closer. The same weathered, worn-looking face, with sharp-angled features of her nose and jawline, the scraggly short chin-length black hair. The saucer-like eyes, dark as the night sky Sophie was sitting under. The shrill voice speaking words repeating in each dream, "Did you find the key?" She heard the words echoing again in her mind. The dream that had been going on for a few weeks now. Too frequently. Always the same question. There were three things she had to find out. Who was this woman? Why was she haunting her dreams? If the words were a message, what did it mean?

CHAPTER 2

Face bursting through the water, she came up like a submarine with a gasp for air. The water trickled off her swim goggles. She turned and headed back under water with three laps to go. Down between the black lines of her lane of the Olympic size pool at the recreation center, enjoying the cool water against her skin once she got over the initial shock. No phone, no thoughts, no schedule; just her and the water. Her only focus was on breathing and completing the lap. The experience of growing up with a pool and being on the swim team in high school left her with a lifelong love of being in the water. Above the water, she was surrounded by noises of a few other patrons of various ages, but it was easy to block out the sounds and focus, especially underwater. The world was quiet. This was where she found her peace.

After completing her routine Saturday morning swim, Sophie climbed the ladder out of the pool. Water spilled off her skin and continued to drip until she found her plush, orange with pink striped towel on the bench against the wall and wrapped it around her athletic, hourglass shape. While getting her clothes out of the locker, she noticed a missed call on her cell phone from her boyfriend, Logan. She got dressed, put her headphones on and called him back as she was gathering the rest of her belongings in the bag and carefully wrapping the wet, one-piece navy swimsuit in the towel. The phone rang a few times and then finally an answer on the other end.

"Good morning beautiful, hold on one second," Logan said.

Sophie waited on the line as she heard muffled talking in the background. Heading out of the locker room, she passed the next shift of regular swimmers coming in and gave a wave of acknowledgement.

"Okay, I'm back. Work stuff. What's up? How was your swim?" Logan asked.

"Good. You're at the office today?"

"Yeah, big project and tying up some loose ends. Are we still on for dinner tomorrow night? Oh, actually wait. Scratch that. How about Wednesday night?" he said, checking his schedule. "Yep, Wednesday for sure," Logan said.

"Ok, then. Wednesday night it is," Sophie said.

"I'll just meet you at the restaurant, okay? Have a full schedule that day and some errands to run but I'll meet you there at six, Wednesday night?"

"Six is fine," Sophie said. "Just finishing packing. Not too much left and that should be a light day. I can call and make a reservation."

"That would be great," Logan agreed.

"How's the new apartment? Did you move any of your stuff in yet? I can even start moving my stuff over Tuesday," Sophie said.

"Actually, I've been so busy, and I wanted to ask you something before we get into the apartment," Logan said.

"Ohhh kay."

"Oh, you know what? I gotta go, I have a call coming in from corporate I've been waiting for. I'll see you Wednesday night though, Soph."

Logan hung up abruptly, which was a normal occurrence for him. Sophie had grown accustomed to his busy schedule and constant phone use. He was on business calls most of the day with people all over the country and always moving a hundred miles a minute. She, among others, had considered him the king of multi-tasking. Logan McCoy was a marketing executive. He managed client accounts from all over the country, and the company he worked for was based in New York.

Sophie couldn't help but wonder what the question was. *Is he going to pop THE question?* They were moving in together in a matter of days. They had been together for a few years already. *Is it too soon? That would be the logical next step, right?* They were both engineers of their future and had always stuck to a perceived timeline of life events. College, career, long-term relationship, marriage, family, travel, retirement, grandkids, etc. They just assumed there was an order to things. A natural order to follow to maximize the enjoyment of life. Sophie was lost in thought by the possibility of an engagement in her near future. She was excited in part, but also had some reservations at the same time. She pushed past the doubt. This was the path she created and wanted. She remembered how happy Harlan and Grayce were at the party and the bond they shared with being together so many years. *Maybe they didn't start out perfect either.*

She arrived home and switched gears to get ready and go meet another one of her clients, Maxwell Russo. She had been working on a design for his waterfront condo. He wanted a few of his rooms updated with a modern flair. She was prepared to stop by his house and drop off some sketches and samples for him and discuss which options to go with.

Her part-time employment with the Harbor View Psychological Center was winding down. She had given notice a few weeks ago after interviewing for and accepting a full-time counseling position at a new private practice. Sophie was looking forward to taking a position that she had been working

toward for the past several years. The side work she was involved in was also rewarding, but not part of her original as-
pirations. She enjoyed dabbling in interior design, at least for
the completion of the next project. She liked the idea of working with color and textures, creating unique spaces to fit the
client's purpose. In addition to the creativity, she welcomed
the lighter side of the job compared to the weight of the problems of the human condition. Her skills as a psychologist
crossed over into this field with color theory and working with
the client one on one. Most had no problem opening up to her
and sharing their life stories along with any issues they had
encountered along the way, sensing a good listening ear. One
of the contrasting things she enjoyed about design work was
the closure. There was a point where the job reached completion, which gave more of a concrete sense of accomplishment,
as opposed to a more complicated, continuous work in progress of psychology. Even still, she enjoyed her patients, and
they were each unique beings with some type of imperfection.
She was grateful to be able to help them in some small way.

After a quick shower, there was still time for breakfast
since she didn't have to be at Max's condo until noon. The few
pans she had were not yet packed, so she scrambled an egg in
a small cast-iron skillet and added it to cheese on wheat toast.
She washed it down with her usual morning coffee, which
wasn't coffee at all, but ginger ale and orange juice. Although
the smell of coffee was inviting, she never liked the bitter taste
of it. She considered soda a much more suitable choice in the
morning.

Clearing a few boxes out of the way, she reached for one
of the chairs that was vacant and sat down at the small square
kitchen table, furnished by the landlord. The 500-square-foot
apartment, seemingly smaller now, was cluttered with both
packed and half packed boxes. Sophie hadn't acquired that
many belongings in her 35 years, especially moving around,

but things multiply quickly once you start taking them out of cupboards and closets.

After breakfast, she changed out of her short, satin, black robe, into one of her favorite outfits, which consisted of tall brown riding boots, gray leggings, and a cream color long sleeve knit shirt. She added a lengthy, sleeveless, navy-colored over wrap, open but casually bloused in the front. Sophie completed her look with a subtle plaid-patterned light blueish gray, navy and tan scarf. A comfortable fall outfit that was also suitable for weekend professionalism. She put on a light covering of neutral-colored makeup and threw her medium-length, brown hair in a clip and pulled a few pieces from the layers out on each side, slightly framing her face, and finished off with a soft spray of subtle, citrus-scented perfume. She headed out the door to the client's waterfront condo.

Sophie had known this particular client for many years, being the older brother of her best friend. He was also a good friend of Harlan Reed. He referred Harlan to Sophie. Max was a divorced attorney in his late 40s. He had helped Sophie with some legal advice in the past. She had guided him with some advice regarding relationships and dealing with his ex-wife in trade.

Max greeted Sophie at the door, dressed in a much more casual outfit than she was used to seeing him in. Although she had seen him several times over a number of years, he was usually coming from or going to court. The jeans and dark gray hoodie he wore contrasted with the suit she normally saw him dressed in. Max welcomed her in and made room at his oversized dining room table. He shuffled his laptop, tablet, files, and yellow legal pads around to create space for the samples Sophie brought. She set the small black portfolio containing her sketches on the table and unloaded the flooring, carpet, and paint samples. Sophie presented the drawings for each room. She suggested colors and patterns that would improve the overall aesthetics of the home, taking his wishes and previous input into consideration. Max was pleased with the designs. He requested a couple of small changes, they scheduled a tentative date for install, and the meeting was finished.

"Did you eat lunch yet? I was going to run up to The Bistro and see Marcella. She's working today. You want to join me?" Max asked.

"Actually no. I mean, no, I haven't had lunch. I had a late breakfast."

"A girl has to eat lunch. Even something light? They have salads. They even have water, if you're going extra light. Besides what else do you have to do today? What better thing to do than spend it with us?" Max said.

"Uhh, well, I have to finish packing. Those boxes aren't gonna fill themselves."

"Ahh, that can wait. What do you have, like 10 boxes?" Max said, holding up his hand, lightly dismissing the task of packing.

She wouldn't mind surprising her friend Marcella, or Ell as she usually called her. Plus, Max was always entertaining and pleasant to be around. Maxwell and Marcella Russo were as close to Sophie as family could come without being blood related. She had known them both for some time, being friends with Marcella for twenty-plus years. Marcella's bubbly, outgoing personality welcomed Sophie the first day they met, the summer that Sophie moved into the neighborhood. Marcella, having many acquaintances, made the transition to the new school bearable for Sophie that fourth-grade year.

"Alright, ya talked me into it. It would be nice to surprise Ell at work."

"Great! It's a date!" Max said playfully.

"Not a date, Max." Sophie rolling her eyes in amusement.

Max was always very personable and playful. Even though he never had kids of his own, he was always involved with his nephew Sam, Marcella's eight-year-old son. Sophie respected how he took care of Marcella and her son after Sam's father was out of the picture. Max was the protective big brother, being fourteen years older than Marcella. Even though it wasn't his responsibility, he made sure they had whatever they needed. They were very close and involved in each other's lives. He definitely had the means, which made it that much more possible. Marcella always appreciated whatever he did for them. Being a single mom was not without its challenges. She was completely capable of handling it all but knowing she could depend on Max to help out was comforting.

When it came to his personal life, he would probably take out any woman who agreed to his company on a date. Since his divorce, he had bounced from girl to girl, all just casual, nothing serious. Not sure he would ever be tied down again. He was always a gentleman, not to mention easy on the eyes and full of confident charm; all to blame for his busy social calendar.

After being seated at their table by the host, Marcella came bouncing over. She was surprised and excited to see them both. Sophie and Max exchanged a familiar smile at Marcella's excited, high-pitched greeting that was more comical and heartwarming than annoying. After a few minutes of catching up, she took their order. Returning with a ginger ale and an iced tea, Marcella sat down in the booth with them to visit. She had a few extra minutes since the guests at her only other table were finished and standing up to leave. Sophie shared the progress on Max's project. Max expressed his approval and appreciation. His younger sister had worked as a server for quite some time and had been at The Bistro for about five years. Her expertise was in bartending, but she took the job that was available. She had a natural connection with people and enjoyed the fast-paced, always moving serving world.

After a few minutes catching up, Marcella looked up and saw the owner entering the building. She was surprised to see him on his day off and mentioned it to them just as another server walked by warning Marcella of the news.

"Well, nice chat but back to work; your food is probably up anyway," Marcella said.

It was quiet after Marcella left. There was an awkward silence for a few seconds until Max's phone rang. It was a client of his that was having ongoing issues with his rental property. Max took the call at the table knowing it would be brief. Max mentioned he was in a meeting and would take care of whatever the client needed first thing after he was done and assured him all would be good.

They finished eating lunch and exchanged pleasant, casual conversation. Max finally checked his notifications on his cell phone that he had silenced during lunch only to find relentless emails from clients that needed various issues taken care of. He wanted to get a jump on things before they got too backed up. After a quick goodbye to Marcella, they headed out to get on with their day.

On her way home, Sophie stopped at an antique mall to check out any interesting finds for the new apartment. She appreciated vintage objects and enjoyed using them in creative ways or incorporating them as part of her décor. Passing by a few tables, she found nothing of interest. After perusing a few more tables, she decided to head home. Circling the last table, she noticed a couple things that caught her attention. She picked up an antique skeleton key about four inches long. The weight of the once shiny and now worn object surprised her, being heavier than she would have guessed. Next to the key was a vintage wax and seal set for letters. The seal had an intriguing pattern with two crescent moons, back-to-back in a web of lines with an edge of half sunbursts surrounding them. The second one in the set had a single feather with textured lines. The third in the set had a Celtic knot. She thought that would be a great gift or even something she could use herself. It was one of those rare finds that spoke to her, and she couldn't pass up.

CHAPTER 3

Arriving back at her apartment in the late afternoon, Sophie returned to the task of packing boxes. She completed filling one of the boxes, sealed it with packing tape, and stacked it in the living room in the ready-to-go pile. In just a few short days, she would be setting the path for her future, moving into a new apartment, and starting her dream job. Looking around at the peeling paint, outdated kitchen, and much needed renovations of her apartment, she was excited for the new apartment and moving to the next level with Logan. They discussed keeping one of their existing apartments and moving in together until an opportunity for a brand-new apartment came up. They agreed that it would be best to find something fresh for both of them. She fought the urge to call the new apartment office and find out if everything was confirmed for move-in day. Logan assured her he would handle the details. He was just as much of a leader of tasks as she was, confirming everything, taking nothing for granted, and she had been so busy and distracted with her patients at Harbor View and the design projects, she didn't mind him volunteering to take the lead on securing the apartment details. She wanted to give him a chance to handle things, and for their relationship to work, she had to trust him. *Yes, that was the right thing to do. Right?*

The rumble in her stomach encouraged her to put those thoughts on hold and break for ordering dinner. Sophie grabbed a takeout menu from the side of the fridge and ordered her usual chicken fried rice. She knew like clockwork they would be knocking on the door in about eighteen minutes; just enough time to get another box packed.

As she returned the menu on the fridge under her pineapple magnet, she glanced at the shelf on the wall by the kitchen table, figuring that was as good a place as any to start. She wasn't a big collector of knick-knacks, but she did have a few valuable treasures that were significant or sentimental in some way. She started taking the items off the shelf to wrap and carefully place in the box. One of the items she removed was a hand-carved wooden turtle. It was small enough to fit onto the palm of her hand but large enough to stand out on a shelf. The light and dark, two-tone stain was beautiful. She admired the carefully hand-crafted lines, running her fingertip over the texture of the turtle's shell.

It had been almost two years since the artist gave it to her. He was one of her patients at Harbor View. A man old enough to be her father or grandfather. He never talked about family or children, so she assumed he was alone or estranged from any family. He never had any visitors, which is why she made sure to spend a little extra time with him when she could. He enjoyed the conversation. She listened to his adventures, sometimes wondering if they were true or perhaps made up in his mind. Things didn't always seem to make sense which was not abnormal for a man his age. He enjoyed woodworking as a hobby. It was more therapeutic for him. He appreciated her theory that depression was a back-up of creativity bursting to come out, and anxiety was a back-up of energy needing to be expelled. He mentioned that made the most sense to him out of all the various things that he had heard over the years in his counseling sessions. He told her that the turtle reminded him of her, and he wanted to thank her for being kind and offering a listening ear.

There was an expected knock at the door. The food delivery was running early today Sophie thought as she opened the door. Instead of the delivery person, Sophie was surprised to see Marcella and her son Sam standing in front of her.

"Hi, Auntie Soph! Look what I got!" Proudly holding up a brown fast-food bag in one hand and a cup in the other.

"Burger and fries?" Sophie asked.

"Yep, and a shake!" Sam said as he playfully shook and wiggled around. He rushed in to hug her. Then past her to the table to get to work on his food.

"Your fav! Come on in, I'll take a fry." He was like a little Max, running around with his same sense of humor.

Sophie turned toward Marcella with a smile which turned to a straight face upon seeing that Marcella didn't look so happy. A switch from a few short hours ago.

"What's up? Everything ok?" Sophie asked.

"I brought wine," Marcella said, holding up a bottle of Riesling.

"Rough day at the office? Or is it motherhood?" Sophie asked just before the food delivery person approached the door.

Marcella went into the apartment, took off her coat, and tossed it on the back of the sofa as Sophie settled up with the food delivery payment. Sophie closed the door and Marcella turned toward Sophie.

"Found out I won't have a job in a few weeks. So, that happened," said Marcella.

"What? What happened?" Sophie set her food on the coffee table and sat on the couch.

"Ugh, so frustrating," Marcella said, tossing her purse on top of her jacket as it slid off and hit the floor. "Ugh!" She rolled her eyes and left the purse on the floor.

"Come sit down," Sophie said, curling her legs up on the end of the couch, motioning for Marcella to sit next to her.

"Yeah, so work was just another day, you were there, everything was fine. You saw the owner came in, which I thought was unusual for his day off. He usually comes in regularly on Thursdays, so we were all kinda thinking something was up. You know, just a strange vibe. So, shortly after you left, he called us all into the kitchen and said that the restaurant was changing ownership. He's bringing on a partner who owns a couple more restaurants. At least one of the restaurants will be closing. Apparently, they are letting most of the Bistro staff go, so the staff from the other locations can transfer. Those are the details I have for now or at least remember. I was shocked and lost track of what he said somewhere in the middle, but I know we can stay for a month or two at most. Definitely by the end of the year, I will be out of a job."

"Oh no, I'm so sorry. I can't believe he would let everyone go," Sophie said.

"They wanna change things up a little. Weed people out and keep some from the other place. They're making some menu changes, and there is talk of changing the name and having a fresh theme. Who knows, the new partner could be kicking in more money and wants things a certain way," Marcella said.

"Hmm, what are you going to do?" Sophie asked.

"No idea, but I'll be polishing up my resume. Which is also why I wanted to talk to you. Can you give me some tips? I haven't made one in several years."

"Absolutely, whatever you need," Sophie said.

"Thanks, I appreciate it. But not tonight. Where'd that wine go?" Marcella asked, taking the bottle from the coffee table to the kitchen. "Did you pack the glasses already?"

"I think they are in the bottom box next to the table," Sophie said.

"I'll get 'em," Marcella said, rummaging through the box in the kitchen.

"When's the big move? You're taking your stuff to the new apartment in the next couple days, right? I'm surprised you haven't been over there every day looking at it, figuring out where everything is going to go," Marcella said.

"Honestly, I have been busy with work and these projects for Harlan and Max. Plus packing. Logan is handling the details with the leasing office. I saw it when we first decided to rent it. So, I know what it looks like. I have a sketch or two of a practical layout, along with some photos," Sophie said.

"Of course, you do. But whoa, wait, letting Logan handle the leasing details! Who are you and what have you done with my friend?" Marcella said.

"I know, keep up with the times. You didn't get that e-mail? There might be more changes after Tuesday night's dinner too. Said he had something to talk about. Well, actually, he said he had a question to ask me before we get into the new apartment," Sophie said.

"Wow! Well, you better call me right after dinner and let me know. If it's a ring, I want a picture. New house and new hardware! When do you have to be out of here?" Marcella asked.

"I have to be completely out by this week. They need to paint and clean and then the new tenant is moving in. I don't have that much stuff, and since it was furnished, all I'm moving is my boxes of stuff," Sophie said.

"Apparently, this is a popular place. I was just talking to someone the other day about this building. I have a friend that tried to rent here, well, you know the girl that cuts my hair. There is a waiting list a mile long to get in. Actually, she was having difficulty finding anything in this area. Several places have waiting lists. There are a few places available, but they are 'crap holes' was the technical term she used, I believe,"

Marcella said as she set the glasses on the table and pulled out the bottle opener. She poured two glasses in clear, stemless wine glasses and took one to Sophie in the living room.

"To new adventures. Salud," Marcella said, holding her glass up.

"Salud," Sophie said as they clinked their glasses together.

Sitting on the couch next to Sophie, Marcella took a sip of wine and set the glass on the end table next to her. She glanced at the picture frame of Sophie and Logan with sand and water in the background. Both wearing swimsuits. The corner edge of the beach side, tiki bar in the Florida Keys showing. One she remembered well. Or at least remembered most nights they spent there. She remembered taking that photo on their trip to the Keys. It was just over a year ago. There were four of them that went on the trip. Sophie, Logan, Marcella, and Marcella's ex, Jake.

"What a great weekend. Sun, fun and lots of drinks. When can we go back?" Marcella said, picking up the picture frame.

"It was fun. And that condo was gorgeous! That was so generous of Max to let us stay there," Sophie added.

"I gotta say, I'm a little surprised that Logan is finally ready to settle down," Marcella said.

"What makes you say that?" Sophie asked.

"I mean, that's great, don't get me wrong, you deserve to be happy. I always thought he was the type that is married only to his job you know? Like when we were all on vacation, but he was preoccupied. Somewhat attached to work still. Like something was pulling him in that direction," Marcella said.

"He is very busy, but I think he is just trying to make a good impression. Trying to work his way up. He has a strong work ethic which is great. Right?" Sophie said.

"Absolutely! That is true and unlike Jake who probably didn't even know how to spell the word 'work.' So, are you excited to move in with him?" Marcella asked.

"It will be different having to share a space, of course. We are both used to having our own thing, our own space. But this next step is like a natural progression," Sophie said.

"Well, see you're starting to sound like him already. A 'natural progression,'" Marcella said, deepening her tone as she imitated Logan's formal-sounding voice then gave a slight laugh out loud amusing herself.

Sophie laughed with her at how ridiculous that sounded. "Oh stop." Shaking her head and rolling her eyes but slightly amused as well.

"Ok, ok," Marcella said, sliding her wine glass off the table, downing what was left, revealing an empty glass. "Refill?"

"That would be quite pleasing. Thank you," Sophie said, with a playfully formal tone.

Marcella paused and glanced around the small kitchen, checking out the packing and spotted the turtle.

"This is cute. Where'd this guy come from?" Marcella said, holding up the wooden carved turtle in her hand.

"Oh, my little turtle guy. A patient from Harbor View. Never had any family or friends stop by. He had a couple visitors, if that, the entire time he was there. He was so sweet. He always had stories to tell but not many listeners. Best part of the job was talking with the people and hearing stories about their lives, although they weren't always good stories. Anyway, he gave it to me one day shortly before he was discharged to go home. A token of appreciation," Sophie said.

"It's adorable! Do you still keep in contact with him?" Marcella asked.

"We emailed back and forth a few times, mostly just follow-up with his treatment but nothing lately. I'll check in with him after the move and see how he's doing. He always had intriguing stories from his time in the military. Sometimes had trouble differentiating between embellished details and facts, but still interesting. He's a warm, charming man to talk to. I hope he's doing well." Sophie said.

He enjoyed talking about his training, his time flying, and even some of the missions he went on as an Air Force pilot. Sophie shared a few of her favorites from the Ezra collection while they finished the bottle of wine along with the fried rice and eggrolls. They hadn't noticed that a couple hours of time passed. Sam had been entertained in Sophie's room, playing games and watching a movie on her tablet. Marcella cleared the dishes from the coffee table and went to check in on Sam. He assured her that he was a big boy now, capable of taking care of himself.

Marcella returned to the living room and settled in on the couch, grabbing the plush, gray throw off the back and tossing half of the blanket toward Sophie. "I thought it was so ironic that a man that flew a plane and solved engine problems literally on the fly had difficulty going to the grocery store or to the bank. Things we take for granted," Sophie said.

"So, he never mentioned a love story in all the conversations?" asked Marcella.

"He never mentioned getting married or having children. For all I know he was a bachelor his whole life. He had a difficult time connecting to people when he returned home," Sophie said, then paused. "Actually, now that I think about it, there was a woman that he mentioned. It was hard to tell if she was his mother or his sister or his wife, possibly? He didn't mention her often but there was some connection there. I sensed some type of sadness."

"What about pictures? Most people keep at least a picture," Marcella said, pointing to the frame on the end table. "But then again, your family wasn't really into that either. No photo albums, no embarrassing pictures of you."

"He didn't keep any pictures or at least he never showed me any. Just stories," Sophie said.

"Sounds like he had the material with all the adventures,

real or imaginary," Marcella said.

"But when he didn't want to share something, he would be very tight-lipped. You wouldn't be able to pull it out of him if you tried. I would definitely trust him with confidential information and government secrets. A steel trap," Sophie said.

"Who was the woman he mentioned?" Marcella asked.

"I'm trying to think of her name. It was like Iris or Helen or something. I forget," Sophie said and then paused to search her memory. "I can't remember."

A couple hours later, after her guests left, Sophie was brushing her teeth before bed. While replaying bits of the conversation with Marcella in her head, she finally remembered the name.

"Hazel! That was it," Sophie said aloud.

CHAPTER 4

Everything started off as a normal Monday, as it usually does, until it wasn't. Sophie arrived at Harbor View to find one of the doctors, a nurse, and another staff member huddled around the grouping of chairs in the lobby waiting room. She thought that was a strange sight, even taking into consideration that she was at a psychological center. She had seen some very peculiar things and met some unique people with all types of mental health challenges. As she approached and looked closer, she noticed a man lying on the floor with his head and upper body under the chair. This was a grown adult man on the floor like a child hiding under a chair, and clearly, he couldn't fit his whole body where he thought he might. The staff was trying to persuade him to get up without further upsetting him. He was discharged and waiting for a ride home but apparently didn't consider himself ready to leave. Sophie recognized the man's blue tennis shoes. He was not one of her patients, but she'd had some brief interactions with him. Enough to know that he loved popsicles more than anything on the planet. She remembered he liked the orange ones the best, after passing them out one day in the rec room.

Sophie pulled the doctor aside, as she overheard the nurse volunteering to go retrieve medication to subdue him. Sophie mentioned that she wanted to try something before they defaulted to medication. After failed attempts and wanting to avoid any further escalation, the doctor welcomed the assistance. Sophie asked them to keep him calm and talk to him and she would be back in a minute.

She quickly headed for the kitchen. When she opened the freezer there were no popsicles. *Of course not.* She paused for a minute to think of an acceptable substitute. On a mission, she hurried to the vending machine and returned with a can of orange soda, hoping that would be sufficient. Most of the group dispersed by the time she came back. Sophie got down on the floor and stuck her head under the chair to see the man's face. She greeted him and introduced herself, reminding him of their meeting with the popsicles. After mentioning that they were out of popsicles, she showed him the ice cold can of orange soda hoping that would entice him enough to come out from under the chair. Sophie asked him if he wanted to join her, sitting on one of the chairs. There was a youthful light in his eyes. He moved out from under the chair and the doctor helped him up into a sitting position in the chair. The doctor was called away, but Sophie assured him that she would see the situation through. Sophie sat with him for several minutes before his family arrived.

The topic of ice cream led Sophie to share one of her favorite things to do as a child. She mentioned the excitement when there was even a hint of that familiar chime, heard blocks away. She would find change in her piggy bank and rush out in search of the little white truck with colored menu pictures on the side. Sophie was caught up in the memory; she didn't notice him staring at her. She looked up into wide, icy blue eyes inches away from her. "Do you have the key?"

A sudden bolt of panic transferred from him to her. Ripping her from a pleasant childhood memory into a nightmare. A coolness settling up her back, and at the same time, heat rising in her face making her feel both cold and hot. *He couldn't possibly know about my dream. Why would he ask that?* All she could do was stare back at him for a few seconds until footsteps of the nurse approaching them broke her bewilderment and she handed Sophie a set of keys. "He left these in the room," the nurse said.

Sophie smiled at the nurse with gratitude and swiftly handed them to the man. They both sat back in their chairs with an audible sigh of relief. The man mentioned how when he was little, his dad would bring home popsicles for him and his brother. One of the rare, pleasant memories of his childhood.

After a much calmer send off, Sophie settled into her office for a few minutes before group therapy. She completed some routine paperwork on clients and reports that she needed to catch up on. Harbor View Psychological Center was mainly an inpatient facility. Depending on their needs, patients were able to stay for long or short-term care. They also offered group or individual outpatient therapy programs. Sophie oversaw the group therapy program. She created treatment programs and implemented them in the therapy sessions. One of these programs included art therapy.

A new patient's chart was sitting on her desk with a note. The patient, Simon, was joining the art therapy session today. Sophie ran the sessions a few times a week. The first part of the day was devoted to creating some type of artwork, using various media. The second portion was dedicated to discussing what the artwork represented. Show and tell style. There was no right or wrong answer, just an outlet for expression of their emotions. Most of the patients enjoyed the flexibility of the program. They were free to come back and work on their artwork between sessions.

With her time at Harbor View winding down to the last couple days, Sophie had bittersweet memories as she walked through the hall to the group therapy room. She realized how much she would miss this group of people after she left but was looking forward to the opportunities that her new position would provide. She was given the go ahead to start a similar program at her new job. One on a larger scale. In hopefully, a better facility. She was looking forward to the opportunity of working with and helping new groups of people but wanted to make sure her current patients were taken care of.

When Sophie arrived in the classroom-sized group therapy room, most of the patients were already there. A couple of the seasoned patients were arranging the metal folding chairs into a circle for the discussion. Others were gathered by the one small window in the room. Sophie never liked the room that was allocated for group therapy. Something about it always bothered her. From the musty aroma that hit her nose upon entering the room to the disproportionate size of the window compared to the room size, making it somewhat claustrophobic. The walls, covered in a drably outdated and muted mustard color, did not create an appropriately serene environment conducive to making people healthier. Sophie had volunteered many times to repaint the room at her own expense, providing the labor and materials herself. Since renovations were not approved by management, it remained in the current bleak condition. She stopped inquiring after a while, especially since she often had to purchase materials for the art projects. Supplies being the last thing covered by an already insufficient budget. It was not an ideal therapy room, but it was what they had to work with, and the only other option was the hallway, so they made the best of it.

Jade, with jet black hair, a simple beauty hidden behind heavy black eyeliner and many facial piercings, had a beautiful composition. She knew her way around a canvas. More of an artist than she knew she was. Probably more of anything than she thought she was. For a petite girl, she had a hidden feistiness. Although she was very quiet most of the time, there was a lot going on behind the scenes in that head of hers. She always had a book with her. The kind that looked like it would take months to finish, very well used with roughed-up pages and a curled front cover from being bent around and held open for hours. She didn't say much but when she did, it was very insightful. Sophie knew Jade would be a good person to start the session with to get things moving and break the ice.

"Jade, would you start us off? Your painting is very intriguing." Sophie paused, looking at the painting. "There are a lot of bold color and lines. Dark shapes. Can you tell us about it?" Sophie asked.

Shifting in her seat and quietly clearing her throat, Jade picked up her painting that was leaning on the side of her chair and set it up on the windowsill to display.

"I guess. Um, I was sorta going for something that represented a box." Jade paused, shifted her eyes up toward Sophie and then back at the ground. "Something that makes you feel confined. And these dark spots are like shadows. Shadows in your mind that come out to haunt you," Jade said.

"Like, feeling trapped by your own mind?" a voice from across the room said.

Everyone focused their attention at the door where the response came from. A young man in his early twenties stood in the entry, leaning against the door frame, hands pushed in his pockets, showing trim and toned arm muscles. Dressed plainly in a white t-shirt and light blue jeans, he reached up to rub the back of his dark blond buzz cut. Although he had a slightly rough looking exterior, there was something handsome about him. Jade immediately admired the calm confidence that he responded to her painting with. She was even more taken with his interest in providing a response and that he understood what she was going for.

"Simon?" Sophie asked.

He gave a nod of his head and modestly responded, "Yes, ma'am."

"Join us, we are glad to have you here," Sophie said as she motioned to one of the empty seats in the circle. "Great start. Let's keep going with that." Looking at Simon to continue.

"Maybe you're only trapped in your own mind by the limitations you put on yourself," Simon continued, looking at Jade like they were the only two in the room. He gave her a soft smile.

"Well, I picture a large cardboard box, like one of those appliance boxes, big enough to sit in. And you push your elbows out trying to expand the box and break the sides. But the space gets tighter. More frustrating. Like all your efforts are wasted. Where is it getting you?" said one of the other patients, jumping in with a response and breaking eye contact between Jade and Simon.

"If you get too used to being defeated, some people just give up, accept their fate and become complacent," said another group member.

"Yeah, and each day passes and you're in that same damn box again!" replied another patient with a frustrated tone.

"Or it's like a negative energy swirling around you. Like the darkness of a false sense of reality. That's what it wants. For you to give up or give in and become more hopeless until you lose yourself completely and all aspects of your life are dead," Jade said, slightly insecure that she revealed more than she wanted to.

"That's probably a worse fate than death itself," Simon said.

"So, then the question is, how do you dissolve the chains surrounding you, of your own limitations or darkness or whatever it may be, knock the walls down and step out of your box?" asked Sophie, as she wrote the question in large letters on the dry erase board.

"Maybe it depends on the motivation?" Simon added.

"Motivation levels change each day and that's ok. But what

are some weapons against the box, the darkness, the shadows, the limitations?" asked Sophie.

By the time the hour session was finished, they had only focused on one question and one painting, but Sophie considered it one of the most successful groups she had so far. All the patients were engaged and responsive. They filled the board with several responses. All stemming from five words: Faith, Love, Hope, Inspiration, and Joy.

Sophie's satisfaction after the group therapy session ended was short lived and transformed to more of an ominous sensation on her drive home from work. There was a harshness in the air from the wind breaking through the trees, wildly shifting the branches, illuminated by a full, bright moon in the sky. She was so focused on her patient's state of mind that she didn't consider her own until now. Wondering if she could relate a little more to Jade's painting than she wanted to admit. Perhaps it was the haunting dream still reeling in her mind. The lingering echo of words from the dream. *Did you find the key?* Not to mention the bizarre key incident with the patient in the lobby. Maybe she was overthinking again but couldn't shake the uneasiness. The sense that it was one of those days where the universe might be holding you up for a reason or hinting to turn back. Do not pass or proceed with caution.

Sophie's notification tone went off. She glanced over at her phone nesting in the cup holder of the car as she approached a stop light. There was an email from the new private practice that she was going to be employed with, in a few short days. Her excitement returned as she thought of continuing the success of her existing program and carrying it over to a better facility. The short view of the message on the home screen said, "I'm sorry..." Sophie's interest was piqued, and she had to open the email. She couldn't wait until she got home. She pulled her phone out of the cup holder. The light turned green, and cars were moving. As she started going through the intersection, she heard a horn. Startled by the sound of the unexpected blast of the horn, she looked up and saw a car to her left run the red light, crossing in front of her. She instinctively slammed her foot on the brake and her phone flipped onto the floor near the pedals. Adrenaline rushing, her hands started to shake at the close call. But now the road appeared calm and peaceful with traffic flowing like nothing happened, leaving the charging flow of adrenaline throughout her body in its wake. She was shaken from the near crash that could have ended this night very differently, and the concern for the words in the email. Sophie searched for the closest parking lot and pulled off the road, while trying to calm her breathing and racing heart. Shifting into park, she reached down to pick up her phone. With her hands slightly shaking, she tried to open the email. It took a couple attempts from operator error. She finally pulled up the email and read, then re-read the words.

I'm sorry for the short notice. We have had some recent staffing changes and have decided to accept another candidate for the position. Thank you for your interest in our company and we will keep you in mind for...

Sophie stopped reading the remainder of the email. She replayed the words *decided to accept another candidate for the position*. As if she had difficulty processing the information. The overload of thoughts created a moment of numbness through her body. After the initial shock wore off, she returned her phone to the cup holder to create as much physical distance as she could from the email. She sat in the car for a few more minutes until the need to just get home kicked in.

CHAPTER 5

Lying in bed, Sophie had difficulty falling asleep. She watched the clock change for two hours, switching back and forth from pulling the covers up to her neck to kicking them off her feet and legs. Various topics weighing on her mind were the culprits for her sleep disturbance. Finally, she drifted off at least for a little while.

Cold sweat, clinging shirt, Sophie awoke in a panic in the middle of the night. She opened her eyes, afraid to move even the slightest bit. It was one of those dreams where you are thankful to wake up and realize that it was only a dream. Paralyzed with fear, she was unable to move except for the chill that ran up her spine. She saw the same black cloak and the same woman's face from previous dreams. They were engrained in her mind. The words she spoke were now just a memory but one she had playing over and over in her mind. It wasn't what she said but the unsettling tone she used in her question that had Sophie unnerved. *Did you find the key?*

Making every effort to lift her mind from the fog, back into consciousness, she tried some deep breathing techniques she worked on with her patients, concentrating on slow breaths to distract and calm her mind. As she hesitatingly sat up in her bed, the cold fall air drifted through the window across from the foot of her bed, billowing through the sheer white curtains.

The room was dark except for a light haze coming in from the hallway. Her eyes followed the direction of the breeze, curious to find the source of the glow.

Still troubled by the dream, she froze for a moment not wanting to get out of the warm covers. She finally touched bare toes to the cool floor, hearing the wood creak beneath her foot as she added more pressure. She took another deep breath and slowly made her way into the hallway to investigate. Sophie wasn't sure what to expect after the dream she had, then, shaking her head for being creeped out for nothing, she saw the source was the dining room light. *I probably just forgot to turn it off before bed. Yeah, that must be it.* Reaching to click the switch off, the words *save her* floated through her mind with an echo of a whisper. She was glad to be leaving this apartment soon.

As Sophie sat back in her bed, the vision of the woman's face flashed in her mind again, bringing back the eerie sharpness of her angled face, the short stringy brown-grey hair, asking in a shrill voice, *did you find the key?* The words played over and over like nails on a chalk board, haunting her mind.

Sophie was unsure why this dream had made such an impact on her and left her subconscious so unsettled. It was the uncertainty that the dream brought. It was the unanswered questions that were left. Why was this woman so mysterious and why was the question so disturbing? Was Sophie losing her mind?

She had vivid dreams before. Dreams that were more like reality rather than just an illusion, but not quite this haunting. She could make out every detail on the woman's face, including the stone-cold brown eyes, the age lines on her forehead and creases of her eyes. Sophie figured it was a result of working so closely with her patients and listening intently to every detail of their lives. Each life with a story of its own: celebrations, fears, insecurities, choices, traumatic experiences, and redemption. She sometimes had to work at not taking on the feelings of her clients. She also knew dreams were not necessarily literal but representational. What was this saying? Was she trying to find something more?

CHAPTER 6

1929

EDDIE

The usual warmth emanating from the Blue Owl, contrasting the cool winter, was absent. It was just as frosty inside this evening. The open sign in the window was void of a glow. Eddie Stone was one of the owners of The Blue Owl Bar, along with Macie Brooks and Roselyn Mackenzie. He was alone after closing, clearing tables, and restoring items in preparation for another day. Much of the burden of responsibility fell on his shoulders recently. He accepted that responsibility graciously and believed it was the least he could do given the recent circumstances that had changed their lives. This was his area of expertise. He also knew that he was much better at the business end of matters than dealing with emotions. Especially of those closest to him. Eddie feared the situation went from bad to worse with the new information that came to light, one night ago. Eddie stopped cleaning and sat down with a heavy heart. He poured another two fingers' worth of gin in his clear highball glass, this time leaving the bottle next to him. The crisp sting of pine didn't faze him anymore. With a lot on his mind he had to sort out, he knew he wouldn't be leaving anytime soon. He had to tell Roselyn. He picked up the rotary telephone and started to dial. He hesitated, knowing there would probably be no answer on the other end. He hung up the phone.

So much had happened in the past few weeks. The stress of the business was at its highest point. Someone needed to be the rock to see them through it, with Roselyn's family grieving over the loss of Hazel, one of her children and Macie becoming more distant. Eddie knew he couldn't confess to anyone what he heard the night before. It would make things more difficult for everyone. He had to keep quiet. At least for a while. As Macie confessed to him, having no one else to turn to. He agreed to keep her secret at the time, but now it was too much for him to bear. He found a few sheets of paper and a fountain pen to write down his thoughts. They had to come out. Even if it was just on paper.

I am trying to hold it together for all our sakes, trying to keep things afloat mostly on my own, carrying another burden. One of the biggest secrets of my life that could at any moment pull the last thread and unravel all our lives, even if this letter never finds a reader beside myself or at least not for many years to come. The truth must come out someday. I must clear my conscience. Generations to come must know the real truth and what actually happened that night. The letter I write today confesses that I have heard the truth of that night of the most tragic event in the history of our lives. One night has changed the course of that path we set out on forever. There is no returning to how things once were. It is with great sadness and heavy burden that I write this letter. Last night, she came to me in an emotional panic, exhausted and hadn't slept in days. The dark circles under her eyes and the uncontrollable movement in her limbs demonstrated how unstable and distracted she was. We talked well into the morning, as I washed the glasses and cleaned up from the evening's patrons. She looked like she carried such a weight that if held for another second it would destroy her. I lent a listening ear without judgement. We all had our differences, but we were all like a family or at least at one time it was that way. As her confession began, my hands started shaking like the jitter she had was contagious. Almost like the jitter took the form of a creature that crawled along the bar top into my veins. Pouring a shot of whiskey calmed both our creatures. As she was talking, I had a range of emotions flow through me. Shock for what I was hearing. Sadness for the loss and for her, for carrying this burden. Anger toward her for being a part of the event. Guilt for knowing the truth when the people directly involved don't even know the truth and that would make all the difference, or it might make things much worse. Guilt for being a middleman who is now being asked to keep a secret that could destroy lives of two families that I care about deeply. Families that have ties going way back and have been through so much together. Lately the climate has been somewhat difficult. The most difficult decision was what to do with this information, so I have decided to confess in this letter. It is my hope that one day the reader of this letter not only understands the truth of what happened that night but also has insight into the motivation behind the act and the motivation for the secret being kept. Maybe in some small way can bring the story out in the open in order to start healing and perhaps even create a chance for some forgiveness.

After Eddie was finished writing, he ran his hand through his hair to smooth the dark brown strands. Then, in one long swig, he emptied his glass. He stood up, leaning against the edge of the bar to keep his balance. His wrinkled and slightly disheveled shirt, from a long day, came untucked and he decided it wasn't worth the bother to fix. Taking the letter with him, he went down to the Indigo Room in the cellar and found the wax stamp set and sealed the letter with the stamp. The two crescent moons back-to-back surrounded by a web of lines and half sunbursts on the edges.

The sudden, loud pounding coming from the main door upstairs startled him but he needed to find somewhere to place the letter. Whoever was at the door could wait. He scanned the room and found some loose bricks in the wall. He moved the brick, slid the letter in the opening, and put the bricks back in place. Realizing he left the bottle of liquor out in plain sight, he ran up the cellar stairs, quickly locked the door, and returned to the main bar area to find a policeman knocking on the door.

CHAPTER 7

The ringtone of Sophie's cell phone resting on the corner of her desk silenced and went to voicemail as she walked back into her office. She checked her phone and didn't recognize the recent call number but listened to the recording. Someone from a law firm left a number to return the call. That would be a task for after the group therapy session. She was hoping to make as much progress in the session today as they did in the previous one. She guessed the call was probably a referral from Max for design work. Now that she was back to the drawing board for finding a new position, she would welcome the side work.

After the group, she went to talk with her supervisor to see if she could extend her employment. Since the position she was intending to leave for fell through, she had some extra time. Her supervisor agreed that she could stay on for a short time, meaning a few days, but they planned to make some cuts anyway and were doing away with the art therapy group session. What she didn't know until now was that they didn't intend on replacing her after she left.

Being disappointed that she only bought herself a few extra days, the subtleties of how things were mismanaged over the past few years were coming to a head. Being short staffed, low on supplies, having a lack of funding, she decided it was time to move on.

Remembering that she had a phone call to return, Sophie moved outside to the bench in front of the building to get some fresh air and privacy. She expected to have a new client by the time the conversation was finished, not *be* a new client.

"Hello, this is Sophie Thomas. I'm returning a call from Terrance Sullivan. Is he available?"

"Hello, yes, one moment. Let me transfer you to his office."

"Hi Sophie, this is Terrance. Thank you for returning my call. I'm sure you're wondering the purpose of the call."

"Are you a friend of Max Russo?"

"Oh, actually, I do know him, but no, that's not why I called. Unfortunately, I have some sad news regarding Ezra Stone."

"Oh no, what happened?"

"Mr. Stone has passed away, but he listed you as a beneficiary on his trust. Would you be able to come to my office to go over the details?"

"Me? What about his family?"

"He was specific in his instructions, and you are the only one listed."

"Yes, of course, I can come in today if you like. I'm free later this afternoon?"

"That would be great. I'll see you then. Thank you, and again, I'm so sorry for your loss."

The thought that she was just reminiscing about him and the worry that he could have died alone was too much of a distraction to focus on paperwork and patient files. The paperwork would be insignificant since she was leaving anyway. She wasn't in the mood for lunch, so she ended up driving over to the attorney's office a little earlier than originally scheduled. She thought if he was busy, she would rather wait there than at her office.

After a few minutes of sitting in the tan leather club chair in the lobby with her curiosity building, the receptionist led her down a long, stale coffee-scented hallway with several options of solid wood brown doors on either side. Stopping three quarters of the way down the hall, Sophie was guided into a conference room on the left. Now that her throat was dry from the jitters of uncertainty or the result of skipping lunch, she agreed to the offer of a soda to drink. The oversized conference table and brown leather executive chairs took up the entire space. The room gave off a peaceful vibe, with the neutral-colored walls blending into the coordinating abstract painting. She sat for the better part of five minutes waiting, thinking about what she could possibly obtain from the will, or why she was even considered in the first place. Looking around, she was reminded of the last time she was at the doctor's office, waiting with anticipation for news. It was so quiet in the room except for the constant, subtle tapping of the second hand, continually making its way around the wall clock. The door handle clicked and in walked a dark-skinned, mildly stocky man in a three-piece brown suit with heavy footsteps, short black hair close to his head, and decorated with round wire glasses. His crisp ivory shirt pleasantly contrasted his complexion. Very polite, he warmly greeted Sophie as he shook her hand and offered additional condolences. Then he took a seat at the table opposite her. His fresh, woodsy-smelling cologne lingered in the air. He came bearing a large envelope from which he removed the contents.

After signing a few documents, Sophie was the new owner of real estate on the outside edge of the downtown area. She was to be given free and clear title to a property that was owned by Ezra and his family before him. It consisted of one building sectioned into four parts. There were two upstairs apartment units. The lower portion included a small, boutique-style storefront and a connecting bar that was well known in the area and had been in operation for many years until recently. It had been vacant for some time, so Terrance warned her that he was not aware of the condition of the property.

"We are just about finished. Last thing, the keys."

He removed the remaining contents from the envelope. An old set of keys clanked onto the large wood table. There were four keys situated on an old scuffed up key chain. It was a circle with a bright blue background and a turtle in various shades of green. It was worn but you could make out the picture. Sophie stared at the keychain, her eyes tearing up as she thought about the sweet little old man and how lonely he must have been if she was the one sitting here in the lawyer's office receiving part of his estate. Someone he barely knew.

She wasn't quite sure what to do at that point. Still staring at the keys, Terrance Sullivan sensed her uncertainty. "You know, many of my clients encounter sudden, even unexpected changes. So, you're not alone in that. Just think of the next step you need to take. Just one step. Go visit the property. See it in person."

"Sounds like a good first step."

"After that, you can deal with all the other decisions of selling or keeping it or whatever. There's no rush. You're in the driver's seat. And if you need some help figuring it all out, I can get you the number for a real estate agent that I trust."

"Thank you, I appreciate it."

As she walked out of his office building, she saw the sign for a pub across the street. She headed over to have a celebratory drink in honor of Ezra. She took a seat in one of the high-top stools next to a few other patrons lined up next to her and set down the large envelope filled with the documents she had just signed. *Who knew a piece of paper and some ink could have the power to change the direction of a life.*

CHAPTER 8

There was no telling what Sophie would be walking into. She pictured a dusty, dingy, smelly, cluttered mess. She followed her GPS to the outskirts of the downtown area, just under an hour's drive from her apartment. It was pleasantly surprising how the tastefully incorporated brick paved sidewalks added character to the otherwise plain streets. The lamp posts flanking the streets had small, welcome, seasonal flags on them. Trees that lined the length of the street were full of vibrant red, yellow, and orange leaves scattering to the ground as the wind blew. Hesitation turned into slight excitement to see what the building had in store. According to the directions, it was the last building before the parking lot on the corner. She had her choice of spots in the empty parking lot. As she exited her car, the new morning air had a fresh crispness to it, contrasting the character of the old building filled with so much history.

After surveying its entirety, she determined the bar area would be her starting point, since it was on the end nearest the parking lot. The small storefront was to the left of the bar area. There was a separate door to a secluded set of stairs next to the storefront, to get to the two upper apartment units. Neighbors consisted of a bakery and a secondhand clothing store. A small café on the other end completed the short block.

Sophie snapped a few photos of the building and surrounding area with her phone.

Thick wooden doors, almost as wide as they were tall, creaked as she pushed her weight into them to open. They had been out of use for some time. The room was dark except where the sunlight streamed in, exposing a haze of dust. The contrast of the vibrant sunlight made the fifty-six-degree weather warmer on her skin and nice enough to keep the doors open to let more light and fresh air in.

The inside was cluttered with sporadic, unorganized furniture, some covered in large dust cloths. The only light shining in was from the open door. Toward the back, there was an opening to a kitchen area with a large commercial fridge, an old six-burner stove, and oven. There were industrial stainless sinks in a row. A few scattered utensils, pans, and glasses on the stainless-steel counter left around with a light coat of dust. Cobwebs stretched and particles reflected in the sun as she brushed the curtain away from the window, allowing a little more light in from the back of the building. Finding the light switch on the wall only slightly helped the dim, old lighting.

She took a tour of the hallway to the bathrooms and noticed a door that was locked. *Must be the cellar.* The door to the right of the cellar was an inside door leading to the storefront. The knob wouldn't turn; it was locked as well. There was a pane of glass in the window, but it was mostly covered with paper or a shade of some sort. There was a thin space running down the edge that was at one time clear, but the dust and dirt smudged on it made it difficult to make anything out in the room with the contents crowding it. She heard something on the other side of the door that sounded like shuffling on the floor. Cringing, hoping there weren't rodents, she reached in her pocket for the set of keys. Trying each of the few keys on the ring until she found the one that worked. The lock clicked and she turned the door handle to open it just as she heard a voice behind her.

"Hellooo? Chili?"

As Sophie turned toward the direction of the voice, a large chocolate lab with a bright pink collar was flopping toward her, tail wagging excitedly. Sophie bent down to pet the unfamiliar but friendly dog. Trailing behind the dog was a middle-aged man with salt and pepper hair wearing a tweed sport coat, jeans, and black-framed glasses. He was tall, lanky, and neatly groomed. The kind of guy that ironed his jeans.

"Hi there. Sorry for the intrusion. Hope she didn't startle you."

"No, no problem. She's adorable."

"And curious. Usually, this door is closed on our walks. I'm Jamison Brooks." As he held up a hand to wave. "And you already met Chili."

"Nice to meet you both. I'm Sophie."

"You own the building?" Jamison asked.

"I'm still trying to get used to the sound of that. Yes, I just acquired it. Well, inherited it. Just came to check it out. Wasn't sure what condition it would be in."

"Yeah, it's been vacant for a while. Do you have intentions for the place?"

"Still working on the details," Sophie said.

"This was a popular bar for many years. It was actually an old speakeasy. I have some old pictures of the place. I'll see if I can dig them up and bring them by," Jamison said.

"That would be great. I would love to see them."

Chili perked up suddenly as if distracted by something behind the door to the storefront. She trotted a few feet to the door and sniffed. Scratching lightly at the bottom of the door.

"Well, if you need any remodeling done, I'm in construction. I'd be more than happy to give you a quote," Jamison said, walking over to the cellar door to try the handle. "Love the old architecture in these buildings."

"I'll keep that in mind," Sophie said.

"Best of luck and nice meeting you. Chili, come on, girl."

"You too, enjoy your walk."

As soon as they were out of sight, Sophie headed back to the door to the storefront. The dog heard something too. An animal or something? She hoped it wasn't. *That would be awful to have to get rid of.* She carefully turned the door handle, hair on the back of her neck standing up, imagining a critter or multiples running around the building. If it was an animal, she hoped she could get it to run right out the door. Opening the door, she inspected the area before committing to walk all the way in. It was cluttered with dust cloths over pieces of furniture. There were a few display shelves that were mostly empty. Although the windows were covered with paper, there was some light coming in from the front bay window and on either side of the main door that illuminated the room enough to see.

It was quiet; she stood listening for a minute, scanning the area. She cautiously started making her way around the room. As she passed some of the covered items, she came to an area in the far corner that had a few pieces of uncovered furniture. A couch, a coffee table, and a stand that was set up like an end table. She moved toward the storage closet where it housed two mattresses set up on the floor with pillows and blankets on them. Sophie turned and scanned the room again. There was a tall, framed mirror leaning against the wall. Just then she caught a glimpse of a face staring back at her. It wasn't hers. She about jumped out of her skin until she looked closer, and the height of the figure was only a few feet tall. Curly long hair. It belonged to a scared little girl hiding in the corner. Sophie didn't want to make any sudden movements.

"Hi. You don't have to hide. It's alright. My name is Sophie."

She stayed where she was as to not scare the little girl.

Then slowly and carefully, the girl came out from the corner. She couldn't have been more than six or seven years old.

"Hi," the girl said.

"What's your name?"

"Charlie. But it's short for Charlotte," the girl said, relaxing a little.

Sophie didn't have children yet or much experience with them except on a professional level. For some reason, the first thing she thought of was to get the girl some food. She must be hungry. Then she remembered there was a diner at the other end of the block.

"Do you live here?"

The girl nodded her head yes.

"Do you live here by yourself?"

"No, my daddy lives here too."

"Are you hungry?"

The girl nodded her head yes again.

"Ok, let's get some food. Do you want to come with me and sit up on the stool over there?" Sophie asked, pointing to the location.

Sophie pulled out her cell phone and found an online menu with a carry-out phone number on the diner's website. Unsure if it would be safer to leave her or bring her, Sophie decided to take the girl with her to pick up the food at the diner. Plus, it was just down the block. They wouldn't be gone long. The next step was to find the girl's Daddy.

Charlie held Sophie's hand all the way there and back. Sophie didn't want to bombard this little, tiny girl with questions, but weighing most heavily on her mind was where her parents were. Is she homeless? Is she missing? She would find out after they ate.

They returned with the food in what seemed like only a few minutes. Sophie cleared off and wiped down an area for them to sit. She helped the girl up to the high top where they ate grilled cheese, fries, and drank chocolate milkshakes.

"Where is your Daddy now?"

"He went out to get something."

The nurturing instinct in Sophie was satisfied at the moment after meeting the girl's basic need for food. Now the protective instinct kicked in and she was more concerned with the girl's overall safety. *Who is taking care of this girl?* Sophie couldn't imagine what type of father would leave his little girl alone at this age. *Living in a vacant, abandoned building?* She became frustrated. *What a sweet little girl.* She couldn't imagine any sane person doing that. The resentment started to build. *Is he even going to come back at all? What am I supposed to do with her?* The spiral of speculation started. Did he abandon her? Was he an addict going to score some drugs or alcohol? Should she call protective services or the police? It had been a little less than an hour. She needed to come up with a game plan. Obviously, this child needed some care. She decided she would wait another fifteen minutes and then call the police. She questioned why she hadn't just done that to begin with, but something about the girl gave the impression she wasn't in immediate danger.

The couch, across from where they were sitting, was covered with a cloth and had a few items resting on it. Sophie cleaned it off and removed the cover, revealing a surprisingly decent couch, still in good condition. Charlie curled up on the end of the couch. Sophie covered her up with her jacket and sat down next to her. Sophie remembered a hand clapping game that some of the kids at the Harbor View used to play. It was something to pass the time until she figured out what to do or the girl's dad came back.

"Charlie," a loud whisper came from the storefront area. The door between the buildings was open.

"Daddy, I'm in here." They both got up and headed to the store area to find a man near Sophie's own age. He was simply dressed but clean looking for a seemingly homeless man. He was startled to see someone with Charlie, standing in front of him.

"What are you doing with my daughter?" the man asked with concern. Sophie's instant defense set in, along with the questions and frustrations brewing for the past hour.

"What am I doing? Really? I own the building. A better question might be, what are you doing here? Why is this sweet little girl all alone and living in an abandoned building?" Sophie asked, walking toward the man to get a closer view and assess what type of person she was dealing with.

"Did you call the police?" the man asked with more disappointment than anger.

"What? No, I haven't. I wasn't even sure what was going on, and I was preparing to give you a piece of my mind. I didn't think the police should be here for that."

He half smiled, amused by her comment. Although the anger and frustration was directed at him, he appreciated that this stranger took an interest in the safety of his daughter. He also found her initial confidence—and how it turned to slight fluster after seeing him—charming.

In an effort to maintain her composure and not let emotions get the best of her, she attempted to listen and not jump to conclusions, letting her training kick in. She was trying to process the situation but was having difficulty. This was something that should be clear cut, black and white, an easy decision. For the past hour, various images of toothless, grubby clothed, smelly, high, or alcohol-scented men popped in her head. She was surprised by a clean cut and irritatingly good-looking man standing in front of her, with his unsoiled gray t-shirt fitting a toned upper body in all the right places and great-fitting jeans. She could not figure out why she was a bit flustered, and it became more annoying. He should be exhibiting that behavior, not her. This was her building. *Stop looking at the way his shirt fits his shoulders and chest. What is that smell? Soap? Cologne? Enough!*

"Thank you for not calling the police. And thank you for taking care of Charlie," he said.

Sophie sensed the genuineness in his brown eyes and a vulnerable sound in his voice that was somewhat likable, adding to the appeal of his slightly grown out, light brown buzz cut and stubble on his face.

He spotted the leftover food in the bag on the counter.

"Grilled cheese?" he asked.

"Uh, yes. We just grabbed something from down the street. Actually, there's another sandwich in the bag if you want it."

Walking over to open the bag, he took her up on the offer.

"Are you planning on selling the place?"

"I'm still figuring things out, but that is the direction I'm leaning toward. How long have you been here?" Sophie asked.

"About a month." he said, taking a bite of the sandwich. "We will get out of your way. But can you give me a few days to find somewhere else?" he asked.

He was pleasant but cautious, concerned with whether or not he would be able to find somewhere for them to sleep tonight spur of the moment. Something told her not to push at that moment. They had no alternative. It was cold outside, and she couldn't bear the thought of that sweet girl out on the street. Sophie glanced over at Charlie, sitting on the couch, now wearing Sophie's jacket. Ultimately, it wasn't her responsibility. She didn't want to enable him either. He was her father and had to come up with something for her. At some point he needed to move on.

"You can have a week or two at most to figure something out. I think that's more than gorgeous. Uh, generous. More than generous." Sophie sped up her pace, hoping to distract him (or herself) from the debacle of her words, praying for his short-term memory loss of the last few seconds. "It will take me some time to clean this place up, but I will be contacting a real estate agent soon and obviously it will hinder the sale if I have squatters living here."

"Thank you. Absolutely, that is more than generous. I can even help clean the place. It's the least I can do for you letting us stay," he said while fighting a smile, trying to keep his expression as serious and businesslike as he could, for Sophie's sake.

"Ok, sounds good. I know where to find you. I'm going to head out for now," Sophie said, finally able to escape.

"I guess I should ask the name of my new landlord then before you leave?"

"Sophie Thomas. And it would probably be good to know the name of my very temporary tenant."

"Justin Knight."

Sophie sensed this was a bad idea. They had to move on, but she knew they had nowhere to go and that was the problem. What if it became an issue and they wouldn't leave? But something didn't add up. Her intuition was screaming. There was more to what was going on and she needed to find out. Or get them out.

CHAPTER 9

The clear blue sky with the sun shining its heat on her face and sunglasses brought a bright energy and warmth to the day. Sophie decided to walk around the area of her newly owned real estate. She hoped the fresh air and exercise might stir up some thoughts and help lay out some viable options for moving forward. With a new decision to make, she let the ideas flow; nothing was too outlandish. *Lay it all on the table and narrow down. Ideas will spark other ideas. List pros and cons of each.* She pondered what use she would have for keeping it. The building needed extensive cleaning, junk removal, repairs, and updates. Plus, what would she do with a bar? She did not have any interest in, or see a need for, keeping it. There was an attached storefront divided by a wall that had squatters living in it at the moment. There were two upper apartment units that also needed cleaning and updating in order to even rent them out. It would be a huge undertaking for her with moving into a new apartment, trying to find another counseling position, and taking her relationship to the next level with Logan. This is the path that she created over the past several years. She was set on the idea that it was the best for her future.

She contemplated selling the property as is. This way she wouldn't have to complete any renovations. The buyer could make the renovations they see fit for the purpose they need. Even if the price was lower, maybe it would motivate buyers. Whatever she made would be free and clear, and she could put that toward her future. A bigger problem would be if the squatters refused to leave, it might take some time, money, and hassle getting them out. They may damage the place in the process. She could contact Max for his help if it became an issue. This was not something she wanted or had time to deal with. Selling the property was the best decision. She was satisfied with that goal. With everything going on in her life at the moment, Sophie didn't have time for worrying about maintenance of a building or even managing it and renting it out as a landlord.

She thought of Ezra. Appreciative of the gesture, she was unsure why he gifted it to her. She visited but she didn't think they were that close. Did he not have anyone else he was close to? She was grateful for the extra money it would bring in and at the perfect time since she may have a wedding to save for.

Terrance Sullivan was very helpful in getting the number of the real estate agent he mentioned. Sophie thought it would be good to at least have the agent view the property and determine a value for listing it. She had more questions than answers right now. The name of the agent sounded familiar. Then she thought of the real estate agent that helped Marcella buy her condo. Sophie had met Delia Parker once before when she went with Marcella to view the condo for the first time. She could picture the colors of the sign and Delia's picture on the sign in the window of the condo, with her long red hair and black blazer.

Sophie entered the number into her phone. It started ringing, then she had a sudden sensation that she should hang up. She didn't have the information handy to give Delia. Sophie wanted to have the address and other information on the property before calling. It didn't matter since it went to voicemail. Sophie left a message with her contact information and let Delia know that she recently acquired a property. She wanted to set up an appointment to discuss listing the property for sale. Now she just had to wait for the agent to call her back. There was nothing she could do until she received the call back and was able to get her questions answered.

Sophie had made it three quarters around the block. She looked up as the teal blue, vintage 1960s Mustang parked in the lot of Magna Auto Repair roared as it started up. The auto repair had the same oversized corner building as she did one block away. She could see how having the lot easily accessible would be helpful for an auto shop. She admired their sleek logo on their sign. A black brushstroke style letter "m" that continued into a line in the shape of the top of a car.

Making her way around the corner to her own car, she was relieved to be heading back to her apartment. Even though it was starting to become more like just a space than her home, with the majority of her things packed in boxes and decorations taken off the walls. That would all be different tomorrow. Excitement was building. There would be a new home, new pictures, and a new beginning with Logan, no distractions. Then she thought of Charlie's sweet little face, sitting on the couch, swimming in Sophie's coat, remembering when she asked if she was cold; Charlie's response was, "No, your coat just smells good."

CHAPTER 10

Evening dinner reservations with Logan were set. Sophie was running ahead of schedule. With slight butterflies in her stomach, her excitement about the new apartment surfaced. If she got ready now, she would have time to stop by and see their new apartment, since it was on the way to the restaurant. Logan had movers scheduled to take his belongings over the day before while Sophie was visiting the newly inherited real estate.

Sophie slipped into an elegant halter top cocktail dress and black heels to match. She curled her hair and, after working at the style a few times, she decided to pin it up in a loose bun, still appearing somewhat formal. She took one more overall glance in the mirror and gave a final approval. One final sweep across her lips with the tube of rosy, red lipstick and she was ready to go. She arranged a taxi to pick her up in case they enjoyed too many drinks at dinner in celebration of a possible engagement. According to her phone notification, the transportation that she scheduled would arrive in four minutes. Enough time to gather her cocktail purse, switch out a few essentials from her everyday purse, and head out of the dimly lit apartment building. The taxi pulled up in front of her as the notification on her phone chimed again. She greeted the driver and confirmed the destination with a pit stop along the way.

The anticipated short ride took an eternity. Especially hitting all red lights. Pedestrians filling the crosswalks may as well have been walking in slow motion. With fluttering still in her stomach, she wasn't sure she would be able to eat at all.

Sophie called Logan to see if he was still at the apartment or if he had left for the restaurant already. She could swing by, see the apartment, and then they could go to the restaurant together. No answer. She decided to go straight to the restaurant since she hadn't picked up her key to the new place yet. There would be plenty of time to see it after dinner.

As the taxi pulled up to the front of the restaurant, she took a deep breath, already able to smell the garlic-scented air from the delicious Italian cuisine. She gracefully exited the vehicle, the driver wishing her luck with her romantic dinner. Sophie entered the restaurant, stunning and confident in her cocktail attire, looking forward to a nice evening and discussing their future together. Lost in thought for a split second, she was thrust back into reality as the heel of her shoe got caught in the doorway and her ankle rolled, nearly landing her on her backside. In an attempt to catch her balance again, she stumbled to the side, planting on her ankle. Shooting pain and the heat suddenly rising in her face with embarrassment. Looking around at the calm restaurant with candles on the tables, white linens, patrons enjoying libations, her momentarily disturbed world did not impact the rest of the establishment. Thankful no one noticed or at least didn't make it obvious, she continued to the host desk where they pointed her in the direction of her table. She was thankful that her heel did not break (foot or shoe). She walked through the aftershocks of pain in her ankle. It was easily ignored since she was more focused on the embarrassment and trying not to sweat with the anticipation of the evening.

Logan was at the table, distracted by his phone. His eyes met hers as she got closer. He smiled pleasantly, offering her the seat by pulling out the chair next to him. He greeted her with a kiss on the cheek and quickly finished up an email on his phone. Then he turned over the white mug on the table in front of Sophie and proceeded to fill it with coffee from the carafe on the table, topping off his own as well. Just then, the server approached.

"Could I get a red wine please? House is fine. Thank you," Sophie added as the server nodded and walked away to fill her request.

Logan never could remember what type of beverage she liked or didn't like in this case. Sophie thought coffee was an odd choice of beverage for a celebration.

"How was your day? Everything go good with the property?" Logan asked.

Trying to keep things short in hopes to discuss the apartment or any other surprises he may have had.

"Yes, it went well. A couple of small issues to deal with, but I already contacted an agent to list the property. I think selling it would be best. Fewer headaches. You know?" Sophie said.

"I get it. It's a lot for you to handle," Logan said.

The server returned with a tall, sleek wine glass and set it in front of her. Enough of a distraction for Sophie to ignore the hint of condescension in Logan's comment. Sophie took a sip of her cabernet. Setting it back on the table after a few long seconds, she took control of the conversation, since waiting for him provided no results.

"I almost stopped at the new apartment on my way over here. I called, but you must have left already," Sophie said.

"You did?" Logan asked.

"Yeah." Sophie paused. "So, what's this question you have for me? You mentioned on the phone?" Sophie asked with a flirtatious smile.

He looked at Sophie and then at the table. Taking a deep

breath, he proceeded with caution, shifting in his seat, and moving his napkin slightly on the table. He let out another breath, more audible this time. He then looked back at Sophie. His nervousness was causing her own to rise. He put his hand on her hand. Was this actually the moment? Was he going to get on one knee? She had imagined how a proposal would go many times. It was surreal that this could be it.

"Ok, so you know how sometimes things come up unexpectedly and they can be great if you give them a chance? It may seem like deviating from an intended goal or taking a detour, but could work out to be the best thing?"

"Ok. I'm intrigued now," Sophie said.

"Well, a new opportunity came up. The project I have been working on was a success. I was offered a job in New York," Logan said.

"Oh, that's great! Congratulations!" Sophie said.

"I have decided to take it. It's a really great opportunity for advancement that I can't pass up. I have been meaning to tell you but have been fervently working on getting the details for the past couple of weeks." Logan said.

"Couple weeks? You found out about this that long ago? You could have mentioned it then. Why wait until now?" Sophie asked, pulling her hand out from under his.

"I know. I know. I'm sorry, I have been swamped with finishing the project and getting everything situated. I was waiting for the right time to bring it up. You were busy with your work and the interior decorating," Logan said.

"Not too busy to talk about this. Not to mention I am supposed to move into the new apartment tomorrow. So, when are you supposed to be in New York?" Sophie asked.

"Well," Logan paused. "That's the thing. I had the movers pick my stuff up yesterday. I had them scheduled already for the new apartment, so I just changed the destination. Otherwise, they were booked up for several weeks. It all happened so fast. I was able to find an apartment but had to act quickly. I have to be at a meeting in two days. Another big project starting," Logan said, shaking his head as if he believed there was nothing he could do.

"So, what about OUR new apartment?" Sophie asked.

"Unfortunately, with all the craziness going on, I never had a chance to follow up with the lady to finalize the leasing details. I assumed that you could just stay in your apartment. Just renew the lease," Logan said.

"Well, um, I can't stay in my apartment. Might be awkward when the new tenant moves in next week," Sophie said, sick with regret that she left the details of securing the apartment to him.

"Maybe another unit then?" Logan suggested.

"Actually, there is a wait list for my building and pretty much all buildings in the area," Sophie said with frustration.

"Oh, I didn't think it would be a big deal to find a place," Logan said.

"On this short notice? Probably something we should have talked about a little sooner," Sophie said.

"I'm sorry this puts you out. Really, I am. I care about you. But what am I supposed to do? I have an opportunity of a lifetime. Do you expect me to put this opportunity on hold or pass it up?" Logan asked.

"Definitely not, but you could have been honest with me and communicated what was going on," Sophie said.

"Ok." Logan paused and had an expression on his face like there was more. Like the bandage wasn't fully ripped off yet. "Full disclosure. I will be completely honest if that's what you're looking for."

Sophie braced for impact.

"I have been working closely with the people on my team. Long days and nights to complete this project, which you know," Logan said.

"Yes, I'm aware," Sophie said.

"Through the time spent on the project, I found out one of the girls and I have a lot in common. She has also been offered a position in New York. We've decided to share an apartment to cut down costs. There's no sense in both of us paying living expenses when we will probably be working together a lot anyway. I wasn't sure how to tell you," Logan said, bracing for an explosive response.

"So, putting it off until the very last minute was your strategy?" Sophie asked.

Sophie had to laugh at how ridiculous this all was. This work-driven professional communicates all day long, but he is afraid to have a conversation with his girlfriend, who at this moment just became his exasperated ex-girlfriend. She grabbed her wine glass off the table, sat back in her chair, and pondered the conversation. Maybe it was the wine, but somewhere deep down there was a hint of relief. Even with the unknown near future, the frustration and betrayal welling up inside her, she had a small amount of sympathy for him. He couldn't see a problem with how he handled the situation. He really believed there was nothing he could have done to prevent this. That this was his path he was supposed to follow and collateral damage along the way was not his problem. It would be selfish for the other person to get in the way of potential opportunities for him.

After downing the contents of her glass and carefully setting it back on the table, she mustered up every bit of courage and decency. She pleasantly smiled at him. In one motion, she slid her chair back and stood up. Sliding her purse off the table. She turned toward Logan.

"I see you have made up your mind and I wish you all the success you dream of. Thank you for the wine. Thank you for the time we have spent together. It has taught me about the character of people. I am not going to chase someone who doesn't see my value."

Sophie turned, walked away, and didn't look back. Although she could imagine the surprised expression on Logan's face, and that was enough for her.

When she exited the restaurant, her internal monologue let loose. *Was he a complete idiot or did he think I was? Honestly, I couldn't believe what was coming out of his mouth and that he was trying to sell it to me and be nonchalant about it. Taking no responsibility in the fact that our future together was nonexistent now. I will be homeless in a few days, and he is going to be shacking up with someone from his office. How did I miss what was going on? Were there signs? What the hell do I do now?*

Sophie wanted to walk a bit for the fresh air, even in heels and without a jacket. She paid no attention to the slight pain left in her ankle or the goosebumps on her arms. That was the least of her problems to solve. She walked the rest of the way home. Well, home for the moment. She realized that she didn't have a home now. In that moment she was reminded of Justin and Charlie. The prospect of her new home was just shattered, and her old home was being leased to a new tenant next week. She had to be moved out by the next day.

CHAPTER 11

Why do phones ring at the most inopportune times? A few steps from the front entrance of Sophie's apartment building, the screen of her cell phone read, Delia Parker. Her first reaction was to ignore it and call Delia back later. She paused to get herself together and put her thoughts on the evening's events aside to take the phone call. After a few rings, she decided to answer, knowing she had to move things along quickly.

"Hello, this is Sophie."

"Hi Sophie, it's Delia Parker with Step Up Real Estate. I wanted to get back with you about the property you're interested in listing."

"Thank you for calling. Yes, I would like to get this going as soon as possible. Let me know what you need from me," Sophie said.

"Sure thing. I'm glad to help. Right now, the only thing I need from you is a couple hours of your time to go over some comps and a marketing strategy I have in mind for the property. I will also have a few documents for you to sign," Delia said.

"It does need some clean up, but is there a way to sell it as is? Just not sure I will have the time to give it the attention it needs," Sophie said.

"Absolutely, we can go over all that when we meet up. It would be great if we can meet at the property so I can check out the condition as well. But given the area and the type of property, I'm confident that we will be able to find a buyer. Even if it needs a little TLC."

"Oh, there is one thing I need to mention. There are a couple of squatters at the moment. I'm hoping they will be moving on in a few days," Sophie said.

"Ok, good to know. I'm glad you mentioned that. Squatters can be troublesome and hold up the process at times, but we can figure out a solution. No worries. You may want to consult an attorney if you have one," Delia said.

"Yes. I do know one. I'm sure he'd be willing to help," Sophie said, thinking Max would be perfect for the role.

"Excellent. I will draw up the contracts and contact a couple of potential buyers looking in that area," Delia said.

"I am free tomorrow afternoon. Will that be enough time to get everything ready?" Sophie asked.

"Absolutely. Tomorrow is great. I have an appointment at one o'clock and then I'm free. I can give you a call when I'm done, and we can meet at the property?" Delia said.

"Yes, that will work," Sophie agreed.

"I look forward to meeting you tomorrow, Sophie."

"Looking forward to meeting you, too. See you soon."

Sophie made it up the stairs and into her apartment by the time she ended the phone call. While setting her keys and phone down on the kitchen table, she saw the bottle of white wine on the counter and was looking forward to a glass, or the rest of the bottle. First, she wanted to get out of the black cocktail dress and a take a long, hot shower.

Emphatic about blocking the thoughts of Logan from her mind, she focused on the hot water running over her head and face, hearing the dull ping of the water droplets splashing onto the shower pan. She remembered Terrance mentioned taking just one step. Her next step would be getting loose ends with the building tied up. It would be even better if she didn't have to put any time or money into the place considering her attention would be on finding a new home and finding another counseling job. Even if they had to lower the sales price to reflect the condition of the property, anything she made from the sale was free and clear profit, which would help her out. Thanks to Ezra. She settled in on the idea. She could move on, and this was the clearest choice.

Refreshed after the shower, she slid on a pair of charcoal gray yoga pants. Perusing through her closet, she grabbed her favorite orange and blue, Detroit Tigers three-quarter sleeve t-shirt and pulled it on over a white tank top. Sophie poured that glass of wine and turned on the TV. Suddenly, the thought that she had to be out of the apartment by tomorrow hit like a ton of bricks. She had to find another couch to sit on in the next 24 hours. Until now, she was certain that she wanted to sell. But suddenly she was concerned she may be giving up the best option for a home. At least an immediate, available, temporary home.

It was a short walk to the kitchen to find her cell phone on the table. She searched for Delia Parker's name in her contact list. The call went to voicemail and Sophie hung up. She sent a quick text to Delia, asking her to call. Within a few minutes, Sophie's ringtone was going off.

Sophie briefly explained the circumstances and the need for an immediate housing solution. Delia mentioned the possibility of splitting up the building instead of selling as a whole. She suggested Sophie keep one of the apartment units for herself and sell the other sections as a whole or individually. Sophie hadn't considered that option. The apartment units needed cleaning and some renovations, but it could work as a temporary solution. With several changes in a few hours, Sophie needed an escape from the events of the day. At least she had an option for now and could focus on other challenges tomorrow. At the moment, she was comfortable with the idea of watching a movie and time to relax.

Sophie stretched out on the couch, adjusted the throw pillow under her head, and had just pulled the blanket up over her when her phone vibrated on the coffee table in front of her. A text from Marcella came in asking if she had good news. Knowing Marcella wouldn't let this go, Sophie called her.

"Sooooo, what's the word? Good news?" Marcella asked.

"Well, about as good as your layoff news," Sophie said.

"What? I'm on my way over. Sam is at Max's tonight."

Shortly after the phone conversation ended, Marcella opened the door and entered the apartment holding two wine bottles.

"I come bearing gifts," Marcella said.

"Two bottles?" Sophie asked.

"Well, I thought it was going to be a celebration," Marcella said, shrugging her shoulders.

"I already started celebrating," Sophie said with a hint of sarcasm as she held up her wine glass.

"What on earth happened? I was expecting to be blinded by a big rock on your finger and talking ugly bridesmaid dresses tonight." Holding up her hand, waving the discussion off. "You know what? Just pour the wine and let it all out."

The feelings of betrayal and hurt came rushing back. Sophie reached up to wipe a tear that was welling up and finally let loose. She did her best to explain what unfolded at the restaurant, unable to hold back tears. Saying it out loud and actually telling someone made it even more real, more permanent.

"I just can't believe I didn't see it coming. After years of training in psychology, you think I would have picked up on something." Sophie paused and Marcella let her continue, just listening. "Just so much up in the air right now. It's overwhelming. Plus, tomorrow is moving day and I'm not exactly sure where I will be moving to. I know you can relate to all this. You were going through something similar last year, but you had the responsibility of Sam on top of it all," Sophie said.

"True, but you just find a way to move forward. Hey, do you remember what my mom used to say? She would tell me and Max, things will go wrong. You will have very bad days. Set your worries aside long enough to do a few things to re-group. Clean something, exercise, shower, eat a hot meal, take a nap or..."

Sophie joining in and smiled, remembering the helpful words. "Make a list. Yes, I remember her saying that. Wow, I haven't heard that in a long time."

"Things may not be solved right that minute, but you will be better equipped to handle whatever life throws at you. Anyway, that was her recipe for success. Speaking of which, I'm starving!" Marcella said.

"Actually, I just realized that I never ate dinner," Sophie said.

"Pizza?" Marcella asked.

"Definitely, I'll call in the order."

Marcella continued their conversation after Sophie placed the pizza delivery order.

"Move in with Sam and me. We have three rooms. We can put his toys in the basement, and you can have your own room. It will be fun. Like a big slumber party. You don't even have to worry. Free rent! It will be great. Sam would love to have his Auntie there every day."

"Aww, that's very sweet. Just the offer means a lot. If it comes to that, I may take you up on it. The building that Ezra left me has two upper apartment units. I may keep one of them. I'm meeting with the real estate agent tomorrow, so I'm hoping to have more news then," Sophie said.

"Oh yeah, good idea. Is it suitable to live in? Like now?" Marcella asked.

"I mean, it needs some minor work and a good cleaning, but I can work with that," Sophie said.

"Max is pretty handy if you need some help. I'm sure he would be happy to help you." Marcella winked at Sophie.

Sophie shook her head and gave Marcella an eye roll. "Thanks, I'm sure he would be. You know he's too old for me. Stop playing matchmaker. Anyway, I may need his legal expertise."

"You had a nice lunch the other day though, right?" Marcella asked.

"Yes, it was great, but just business and just friends. Max is great but not great for me. It would be too weird. He's family, like a brother or a close cousin. Plus, if it ended badly, I wouldn't want it to affect our friendship," Sophie said.

"Oh, you know I would be on your side. He's my brother, but you're my girl."

"Thank you for that," Sophie said.

"Well, I know Logan wasn't for you that's for sure. He's too much like you. Well, aside from being an asshole, he's on his own fast track and doesn't consider others. You need someone who will compliment and balance you out. Maybe complicate your life a little. But in a good way. You know, make it a little less tidy. Keep it interesting," Marcella said.

Sophie gave a quick "hmm," acknowledging the observation, not agreeing or disagreeing, but considering it as something she hadn't thought of. "Is it strange that I feel slightly relieved by it all?" Maybe she knew that he wasn't right for her. Wondering if there was a voice inside her somewhere telling her but she didn't listen. "Never mind, don't answer that. Let's just put this aside for the evening."

The rest of the night with Marcella brought Sophie back to her teenage years. A slumber party for her last night in the apartment. Complete with pizza, movies, wine, conversation, and her best friend. It was a great distraction from the uncertainty of her future. Tomorrow she would have to return to the world of adulting and recalculate her direction. At this moment, she had no idea what that entailed. She would have to create a new path, different from the one she had worked toward for the past few years. There had always been security in the known, designed path but she was beginning to see a little freedom with the new possibilities.

CHAPTER 12

1929

ROSELYN

Eddie had just switched from the crossword puzzle to the sports section of the Detroit Free Press when he heard the knock. The headline lingered in his mind that the Michigan Wolverines men's basketball team won against the Chicago Maroons at Bartlett Gymnasium. Eddie opened the door of his bungalow and Roselyn Mackenzie was standing on the other side in her calf length, red flapper coat with satin cuffs and collar. Even at her worst, she dressed with style.

It was all she could do to gather the strength to get herself together and set out to see one of her closest friends and business partners. Several weeks had passed since they last saw each other. She had been barely able to function amid the recent tragedy that struck. He had been taking over more of the responsibilities running the Blue Owl in her absence.

"Well, glad to see it's not another copper again. Come in. Come in," Eddie said, his shoulders relaxing with relief. He gave Roselyn a gentle hug. He noticed her pale skin and sullen demeanor, despite her attempt to push it aside.

"They came here, to your house?" Roselyn asked, frowning with concern as she took her coat off and set it carefully over the edge of the sofa along with her handbag.

"No, no, not here. One stopped by the Blue Owl the other night. It was late."

"Anything to be concerned with?" They sat down on the Queen Anne style buttoned leather chairs opposite the sofa.

"I wasn't sure at first. It was late and I had left some things out. He was pounding on the door. Gotta tell ya, I was sweatin' buckets."

"What did he want?"

"It ended up that they were out looking for someone. There was some altercation nearby, and they were after somebody on the run. Maybe thought they were hiding out. Especially since it was late and the lights were on," Eddie said. "Nothing to worry about. You have enough to contend with. How are you?"

"I'm ok. But I really came to check on you. To see how you're doing. I've been worried about you with all the added work that has been dumped on you."

"Leave it to you Ros to worry about everyone else. This is what I know, and this is my way of helping. These are tough times for you. So let me help you this time. With what I can."

"Eddie, you are a gem. I want you to know how much I appreciate you." Roselyn started tearing up, still set off by any little breeze of emotion. Eddie pulled out a navy handkerchief from his pocket and handed it to Roselyn. "Thank you." Eddie nodded in support. Unsure what to say he sat in silence with her for a moment.

"Can I get you some water? Or something stronger perhaps?"

"Yes, please, just water is fine." Roselyn followed Eddie into the kitchen and took a seat at the table. She took a small sip from the half full glass. "One of the things I admire most about you is your ability to push on. You just do what needs to be done. No questions asked. No complaining. You're a survivor, Eddie."

"You'll push on too and get through this, Ros."

"You know what the worst part is? The not knowing. All the information that your brain attempts to put together to try to fill in the gaps of unanswered questions. Like an endless loop of uncertainty in your own mind. But in the end, it's just an unsolved mystery. No closure."

"I'm here for you when you need to try to sort things out, Ros. I hope you know that. Just give it some time," Eddie said.

Roselyn caught a glimpse of a picture hanging in a frame on the wall. She had seen this picture several times. A close-up view of the three of them, Roselyn Mackenzie, Eddie Stone, and Macie Brooks, taken when they first opened the Blue Owl. She stood up and walked over to the picture. Roselyn always liked that picture because it captured the epitome of friendship, success, and happy times. Seeing that picture this time stirred up different emotions. Times had changed drastically.

"Have you heard from Macie? It's been weeks and I still haven't heard a word. She just dropped out of sight."

Eddie shifted in his seat at the kitchen table and reached up to smooth his hair in an attempt to release some of the sudden tension in his body. "Not much, not much at all." Eddie was searching for the words. Something to remain loyal to Macie and Roselyn at the same time. This is what he was afraid of. Being caught in the middle. They had all been friends ever since he could remember, and they both meant the world to him. He wanted to tell Roselyn everything that Macie shared with him. He was so close. The look of desperation on her face broke his heart. He knew she was in search of answers. Answers that only two people could provide. He knew he could satisfy her curiosity with a few simple words. He just needed to lead in with how Macie came to see him a few nights ago. Everything after that would follow with ease. He opened his mouth to speak but couldn't get the words out. Caught between responsibility and loyalty, he decided it wasn't the right time. Eddie knew that Roselyn needed time to heal, and Macie needed time to come to her senses. Macie needed to realize that she should be the one to approach Roselyn and reveal what happened. He was confident that they would work things out in time. He didn't want to take that chance away from either one of them.

CHAPTER 13

PRESENT DAY

The morning came charging in too quickly after a late night and a couple bottles of wine. Sophie woke up with crusty eyes and sour, wine-dry mouth. She reached for a glass of water on the nightstand, but upon closer inspection found disappointment when it was empty. She also found a pink sticky note with black marker in Marcella's handwriting on top of her cell phone. She had to leave early and pick up Sam for a haircut appointment.

Sophie wasn't as motivated as she thought for it being moving day. Since it was only eight o'clock, Sophie rolled back over in bed and closed her eyes. She pulled the comforter up over her head to shield from the morning sunlight creeping in through the curtains. She wasn't meeting Delia until the afternoon, most of her things were packed except her closet and a few last-minute toiletry items which she knew wouldn't take long to pack. All of her boxes would fit in her car. She would make it fit. One trip. Leaving about an hour drive or less. She calculated that she had about five hours until she had to leave. Plenty of time.

Sophie drifted off to sleep again and woke up to a horn honking outside of her building. She rolled over and took her phone off the nightstand to check the time, thinking it must have only been a few minutes since she put her head on the pillow. It was now twelve-thirty in the afternoon. She hopped out of bed, skipped the shower, and went for the ten-minute freshen up option. Sophie found some comfortable clothes appropriate for moving, quickly got dressed, brushed her hair, and put it up in a clip. Giving it a slight mist of hairspray, she made it look as decent as possible without giving up too much time. Deciding to skip the basic make-up routine entirely, she stuffed her morning grooming items into a black and white travel case with a yellow monarch butterfly on top. She zipped it up and scanned the bathroom for any other last-minute items that needed to be removed.

Since she already booked a hotel room for the next two nights a mile from her newly owned real estate, she packed a bag with essentials and a few outfits. Sophie put the rest of her clothes in garbage bags, sealed up the boxes in the kitchen and living room, and gathered all the rest of her belongings from around the apartment. To complete the process, Sophie gave the apartment a light cleaning. She wiped the sinks and counters and swept the floor, making sure it was at least as clean as she found it.

The apartment building and stairway were quiet. There was very little traffic from the twelve other units in her building, which helped as she hauled everything down to her car and packed it in. It took a few tries and some rearranging to fit everything in just right. She was happy to have an SUV at this moment, allowing for a little extra packing space. Her dark gray Grand Cherokee was filled to capacity and ready to go. It was now one thirty pm. She still had almost an hour's drive. Realizing she better stop for some food, she swung through a drive-thru to grab a cheeseburger, fries, and a soda to eat in the car on the way. While sitting, waiting in the drive-thru line with her window down, she glanced over at her keys dangling from the ignition. Keys swaying slightly as the car inched up in line. In a rush, she had completely forgotten to return the key to the apartment office. After picking up her order, she zipped back to the apartment. Luckily, she was only a few blocks away. Parking the car on the street in front of the building, she ran into the office to return the key and sign the move out sheet. She took one last look at her apartment build-ing. There was nothing left for her there. The plan she spent years investing in, dissolved in a matter of days. She was head-ing toward new adventures fueled with a cold burger and flimsy fries.

CHAPTER 14

It was three o'clock in the afternoon before Sophie arrived near her newly acquired building. She was relieved that Delia called to reschedule their appointment, since her previous appointment ran longer than expected. They agreed to meet the following day, which was more than fine with Sophie. They were able to discuss a few options over the phone, which put Sophie's mind at ease. She now had more time to check into her hotel and stop by the store to pick up some cleaning supplies before returning to the building.

As Sophie approached the door of the old bar that now belonged to her, she shifted the plastic bags of cleaning supplies in her hands to unlock the door. It occurred to her how surreal and new this all was. The stale air pushed through to escape as soon as she opened the door. Inside, it was dark and quiet. She thought it would be a good idea to leave the two large doors open for a bit, letting the light and fresh air in. Sophie looked around and realized there was a lot of stuff to go through. It was mostly old junk that could be tossed in the garbage or donated. It was her responsibility now, and she wanted to clean it up a little before having potential buyers come through.

Things were quiet on the other side of the room, toward the storefront area. There was a door in between the two, but there was no noise or activity coming from that side of the building. Sophie hoped that the squatters, Justin and his daughter Charlie, were able to find somewhere else to go. The quiet was a relief. No activity meant it would be easier to show the building to Delia the next day and it would be easier to sell. She didn't want to have to find out from Max how to evict them either. She had no problem telling him to find alternate housing, but the thought of pushing that sweet little girl out into the cold didn't sit well. But she knew it wasn't her choice. They were the last thing she needed to worry about. She just wanted to focus on cleaning up the place as best she could. She was good at sorting and organizing and making things orderly. That was the idea: clean, small repairs, if necessary, sell off the bar and the storefront. Keep one apartment for herself and rent one for steady income, as Delia suggested. Sophie intended on living in one of the apartment units herself until she found out how the employment search panned out. Then depending on where the job was, she would have time to find another apartment. Then she could decide what to do with both apartments when she crossed that bridge. Right now, the task was to get the place ready to list with Delia.

Music was always a good motivator for cleaning. She put some ear buds in and selected a playlist. She scanned the whole area and found a starting point for the cleaning. She had a method, a system for tackling each of the areas by designating an area toward the rear for each category of things to go through. She could use the floor space to separate piles of garbage, donations, items to sell, and items to keep. It was a lot to clean and even though it wasn't her mess to begin with, she didn't want to pass it along to someone else. When Sophie mentioned the items left in the building, Delia suggested she declutter as much as she could to make sure it was in proper order for the photographer to take pictures for marketing the property.

Sophie uncovered years' worth of dust from the cloths that were draped over a few tables in the back toward the kitchen. She decided the table space would be useful for sorting but needed to be wiped down first. She went to the kitchen area to fill up a bucket with soap and water, hoping the sink worked. The pipes made a few strange noises. Both water and air spit out creating a violent, out of sync orchestra sound before expelling brownish water. After running it for a few minutes, it was fine, and the water looked more like something she recognized. Lost in the music and the task at hand, she forgot all about the main doors being open.

When Sophie walked out of the kitchen, her head was down, watching to make sure the water in the new red bucket didn't slosh out. Two dark figures were spotted in her peripheral vision across the room as she lifted her head. She froze in her tracks, hoping they wouldn't see her. Focusing on the two men, both wearing dark clothes, she could smell the cigarette smoke they emitted from across the room. The taller one was wearing a dark blue baseball cap and the other, shorter and stouter, was wearing a black beanie. His round white face stood out between the dark clothing. They were rummaging through the room. Baseball cap guy was digging through her purse, tossing unwanted contents on the bar. The other, lifting dust cloths and quickly searching for items of interest, perusing through the other half of the room. With a sudden jolt into overtime, her heartbeat pounded so loud, she thought they would hear it before they saw her. She had half of a second to come up with a way out. Too late, she was spotted. Sophie mustered up all the courage she could. She stood up taller, took two steps forward changing to a wider stance and spoke from deep within her diaphragm. Forcing a louder than normal voice.

"Can I help you?"

Beanie guy slowly started walking toward her. With a

menacing glare and tone of voice he asked, "You here all by yourself?"

Sophie had a gnawing pain in the pit of her stomach. "There's no money here if that's what you're looking for."

"OH, we're just talking right now, honey. You should really lock your doors. Anyone can just wander in here. Could be dangerous," baseball cap guy said, slurring a few words.

Beanie guy made a sarcastic comment under his breath that she couldn't hear from across the room but the other one snickered, so she figured it wasn't good. Slowly and calculating, they both moved closer to her. She knew this wasn't a good situation, and she had to think of something quickly. There were two of them standing between her and the exit. Her fight and flight were having a debate while she was waiting for the outcome. There was really nowhere to run. *Was there an exit off the kitchen?* She could run back into the kitchen since it was closest, but that would only trap her in a smaller area. A darker area. She knew that wouldn't work. The only thing she had to fend them off was the bucket of soapy water. They had both made their way across the room and were closing in on her. She yelled for help and instinctively threw the bucket at them. The bucket slammed on the floor and the soapy water splashed all over, spreading out to puddles but it had no effect on her pursuers. They were still charging toward her. Sophie pulled one of the tables in between her and her assailants. She attempted to grab anything else within her reach to separate her from them. A thick, sweaty, sandpaper textured hand clamped onto her arm. She thrusted her arm straight down, separating the man's grasp on her. As she turned back toward the kitchen and reached for one of the other tables, her foot slid sideways on the soapy water. She went to catch herself on the table, but her hand slipped off the corner of it. The side of her forehead whacked the table as she was falling to the ground. After a few seconds, the fog lifted from her slightly blurry vision and she was able to make out a third man running in from the front door. That man had a black jacket covering a white shirt and blue jeans. Sophie knew she recognized him. The one she recognized had the man with the beanie on the ground in one swift move. A sweep of the leg, using the water-covered floor to his advantage. Something in the way he handled the situation, moving so fluidly and gracefully, gave the impression that he'd had some sort of training. The man with the baseball cap, assessing that either it wasn't worth the fight, or he was outmatched just gave up and ran out. The man with the beanie scrambled to his feet and stumbled out as fast as he could.

Things happened so quickly, it didn't sink in until after the two men scrambled out the door that the squatter was the third man that rushed in and rescued her from what could have been an even more dangerous situation with an even worse outcome.

Justin chased the men out and came back to help Sophie up just as she was getting to her feet. "Are you ok?"

"Yeah, yeah, I'm good. Thank you so much. I can't imagine...if you hadn't come in when you did," Sophie said.

"Downside is, as you can see, we haven't found another place yet."

"That doesn't even matter right now, I'm just thankful you were here. Talk about perfect timing. That could have gone a lot differently. Thank you."

"My pleasure," Justin said.

Charlie peeked around the corner to see if it was alright to come in and entered with a large chocolate lab right beside her. Jamison Brooks also entered right behind Charlie, guiding her to her father.

"Is everyone alright? Do we need to call the police?" Jamison asked.

Sophie, looking toward Justin, concerned that the police

may ask more questions than he was ready to answer, decided against the idea. "No, we are alright, and nothing was taken or damaged, so there is no need."

"Your head is bleeding. Maybe you should get that checked out," said Justin.

Sophie started to feel a throbbing pain kick in that was masked by the adrenaline moments ago. She reached her fingertips up to the side of her forehead lightly to assess the injury.

"No, that's ok. Really, I'm fine. Just a scratch," Sophie said.

"My wife is a doctor. Why don't you come to my house for dinner tonight? She can take a look at your head. Plus, we are practically neighbors now. I don't live far from here. I found those old photos that I wanted to show you," Jamison said.

"Are you sure your wife wouldn't mind a guest showing up unannounced?" Sophie asked.

"It's no trouble. Your family is welcome too," Jamison said.

"Oh, we aren't together. This is Justin and his daughter Charlie." Sophie wasn't sure what else to say or how much to reveal about the squatters.

Justin started the conversation to break the tension. Reaching out to shake Jamison's hand. "Justin Knight. Actually, we have been staying here in the building for the past few weeks. Sophie didn't know we were here until we met the other day. We hope to be out in a few days, though."

"Oh, well then, the more the merrier. Please join us. It also looks like Chili might enjoy the company tonight," Jamison said, pointing to the lab getting unlimited attention from Charlie.

"Well, a home-cooked meal sounds great. We accept," Justin said.

"Agreed," Sophie replied.

"Alright then! I'll call Mae and let her know we have three more joining us."

CHAPTER 15

The Grand Cherokee was barely stopped in the circle drive-way, and Chili was the first to bust out of the car while giving a bark of recognition of the Brooks' residence. Charlie was next to rush out, trailing behind Chili and following her up to the porch of the craftsman style home. As she shut her car door, Sophie was pleasantly surprised at the curb appeal of the home in front of her. She had always appreciated these styles of homes with the wide-based pillars, the large, covered porch, and the levels of stonework on the face. The dark taupe paint and neutral color stone was a pleasant contrast to the white trim.

Justin caught up with his daughter and joined in giving Chili some greatly appreciated attention. Jamison led them through a wide, modern lined mahogany stained door into a cozy foyer with thick, decorative Mission-style door casing leading them to the rest of the tastefully decorated home. A moderately sized chandelier light fixture above the entry was dimmed, giving the foyer a welcoming soft glow. As soon as they entered, the scent like that of a Mexican restaurant en-ticed their senses. As the four of them made their way into the living room, the black and white photographs and colorful ab-stract works on canvas neatly arranged on the walls created an eye-catching focal point. Chili trotted in further to greet her owner. Charlie followed behind Chili.

An average height woman with a petite frame glided into the living room. She was wearing a gray and white striped apron and her long silky black hair tied back in a ponytail. The angles of her facial features differed from the softness of her personality.

She leaned down and reached to greet Chili. She spotted the little girl coming to join them.

"Well, hello there. I see Chili made a new friend."

"I'm Charlie."

"Hi Charlie, it's very nice to meet you. I'm Mae," she said softly.

Charlie reached her little hand up slightly, taking Mae's hand to accept her greeting. "Hi. I like your hair," Charlie said, intrigued by her satin, black ponytail.

"Oh, thank you, sweetie. You have very pretty hair too. Beautiful curls."

"Thank you," Charlie said.

Mae stood up to greet the other two guests.

"Mae, this is Sophie Thomas. She is the new owner of the old Blue Owl Bar, and this is Justin Knight. He's Charlie's father. They are..." Jamison trailed off, unsure how to label the two of them.

"Guests of my building," Sophie said. "Temporarily, at least."

Mae greeted them warmly and after an exchange of pleasantries, there was a brief awkward moment of quiet. Sophie noticed Mae and Jamison exchanging an uneasy gaze. She thought maybe Mae was confused about the introduction or was overwhelmed with having extra guests spur of the moment. To break the silence, she added, "What smells so delicious, Mae?"

"Chicken enchiladas. Jamison's favorite," Mae said.

"Sounds great! Thank you for having us," Sophie said.

"Oh, you're very welcome. They should be ready in a few more minutes," Mae said.

"Why don't you all come in and have a drink first," Jamison added.

"Sounds great," Justin said.

Jamison led the guests into the back half of the house where an impressive great room with a vaulted ceiling and large uncovered windows led to a serene view of a wooded landscape. The large kitchen island was a perfect spot for housing all the dinner necessities while entertaining, including a full spread of toppings for the enchiladas.

"And I'll take a look at your head, Sophie. I'm sure you're fine, but let's clean it up a little. I insist," Mae said.

"Ok, sure." Sophie followed Mae to the kitchen. Mae guided her to one of the stools at the island. Sophie laid her hand on the cold granite countertop to support herself while adjusting the solid seat beneath her. Mae brought over her moderately sized, brown leather first aid kit and took out a few gauze pads. She bundled them together and squirted some liquid antiseptic on them. Sophie thought the next few seconds were not going to be good, but she held in her resistance.

"You got a good one here, but at least you don't need stitches," Mae said. She cleaned up the wound and placed a bright-colored character bandage on it. "This is the real healing power," Mae said, hinting toward the colorful bandage. "Just let me know if you have any nausea, trouble with your vision or headaches, well other than the pain from the injury."

"Thank you," Sophie said.

Charlie initially stayed behind to play with the dog. Chili, excited she had a playmate, brought a bright green flex ball and dropped it in Charlie's small hand. By now they spilled out into the family room, needing more space. Justin and Jamison took a seat at the far end of the long dining room table, a thick, sturdy, Mission-style table following suit to the rest of the home. The ladies could overhear Jamison asking about the two men that entered the building, uninvited, that Justin chased away.

"And where did you learn those moves?" Sophie asked.

Justin hesitated to answer for a moment. "Military."

"Oh, were you an Army guy?" asked Jamison.

"Marines," Justin answered.

Sophie knew there was more to the story, but she didn't want to pry considering they had all just met. Justin's short, one-word answers also gave a clue that he might want to change the subject. Jamison's cell phone buzzed on the sideboard, home of the catch all, including mail, keys, piles of papers, and other miscellaneous objects. Mae was closer to the phone and picked it up to answer. Sophie noticed after an initial warm greeting, Mae's tone changed to a cold, monotone, subdued sound. She turned her back to Sophie and lowered her voice as she spoke into the phone.

"I already told you no. And this isn't a good time," Mae said into the phone.

Jamison came into the kitchen to get more ice for his glass. The smile on his face quickly turned to a look of concern when Mae's actions hinted it wasn't a pleasant phone call. He moved around in front of her and asked, "Is it him?"

Sophie wasn't sure if she should ask if everything was alright or give them a minute. She didn't want to be an intruder in a private conversation. She stood up and washed her hands at the sink and went to join Justin at the table. A few seconds later the conversation was over, and they both came to join Sophie and Justin at the dining room table. They appeared a bit distracted but were attempting to act normal. Clearly there was something that disturbed the air and left Jamison and his wife visibly unsettled. Jamison brushed it off as an insubordinate construction worker but the expression on Mae's face told a different story.

There was a flash of bright green and then a slight thud on the walnut-colored wood cabinet at the end of the dining room table housing the vintage-looking fine china dinnerware. Next came the sound of canine nails unable to grip underneath her as she made her transition from the carpet to the dining room wood flooring.

"Careful Charlie," Justin said.

"Oh, she's fine," Jamison added. "Plus, they aren't my dishes." He gave Mae a playful glance.

Sophie commented on how lovely the dishes were and mentioned some she had seen at the antique market that Mae would appreciate.

"Those were my grandmother's at one time and passed down to me. She was from the Philippines. She grew up without much money. Apparently, this was something that she had always wanted and finally was able to get them. Or they were given to her as a gift," Mae said.

"Wow, now there is a reason to have fine dishes. I never had anything like that in my family. Actually, we never really had any family heirlooms. Not even photographs," Sophie said.

"Photos are definitely Jamison's family heirloom. We have boxes and boxes of old photos," Mae said.

"Yes, one of my hobbies. Old pictures and photography in general. I have a couple old cameras too," Jamison said.

"Old pictures have a lot of charm to them," Justin said.

"I love the old black and white pictures," Jamison said.

"It's interesting how pictures have changed so much. Not only the advancements but poses. Nobody smiled in the old pictures. But now, big smiles, silly faces, and selfies," Sophie said.

"What would those straight-faced people in past pictures think of silly duck face poses?" Mae asked.

"Ah, I have some pictures to show you after dinner that will amaze you. I have some old pictures of the Blue Owl, back in the days of prohibition. Something to see," Jamison said.

The conversation continued throughout dinner. Jamison talked about his years in construction and owning his own company with all the ups and downs. Mae answered questions about a day in the life of a family practitioner. She kept it both kid friendly and dinner table friendly, no gory details of the trade. Justin shared a couple brief stories about his time in Afghanistan. Trying to keep it on the lighter side, like the comradery and the pranks that they pulled on each other to keep spirits up. Jamison brought up the property Sophie now owned.

"Have you thought any more about having renovations done?" Jamison asked.

"I'm meeting with the real estate agent tomorrow. I'm hoping to sell as is. I will clean it up, but I really don't have the time with looking for a new job to put much effort into it. Plus, the cost of the renovations," Sophie said.

"Well, I just had an idea. It may be a crazy idea but follow me with it for a second," Jamison said.

"I'm listening." Sophie said.

"Ok, what if you keep the bar instead of selling? What if you restore it and reopen it?"

"Hmm. I don't know the first thing about owning or running a bar," Sophie said.

"What if you took on a partner that had money to invest, had expertise in running a business, knew a lot about construction, and had the manpower to do it?" Jamison asked.

"And I'm guessing you have an excellent idea of who that partner might be," Sophie said.

"I have been looking for a new venture. This would be a great project," Jamison said.

"Who would I hire to staff it with?" Sophie asked.

"Well, I know someone you could hire for security. He comes military trained," Jamison said.

"Well, this is a lot to think about. I was counting on the money from the sale. What if you just buy it from me?" Sophie asked.

"That might be something to consider, Sophie. You could still rent out the storefront and the other apartment unit for a steady stream of income. Not to mention the income from the bar itself," Justin added.

"Oh, you're in on this too now?" Sophie asked.

"I have money for the renovations but not sitting on quite that much to purchase it," Jamison said.

"This is a lot to think about. I will say that you have proposed an idea that I wouldn't have thought of or even considered a short time ago. But lately things have been all turned around. Opportunities I thought would pan out didn't," Sophie said.

"Well, just say you will at least take some time to consider it," Jamison said.

"Will do," Sophie said.

After multiple rounds of enchiladas, they moved to the family room to expand to the leather sectional. Charlie found a corner of the couch to cozy up on. Chili laid right up against her, resting her head on Charlie's leg.

"I don't think Chili is going to let Charlie leave," Mae said.

Jamison left to go to the basement; when he found the desired box, he opened it up to verify its contents and dug around the bottom of the box. He found the intricately shaped patterned skeleton key. It was dark metal with highlights of gold. He secured it in his pocket, returned the lid to the box, and rejoined the rest of the party. As he set the box in the middle of the large square, Mission-style coffee table, Jamison's mood of excitement returned.

Sophie glanced around at everyone gathered in the family room. Fire calmly blazing in the fireplace, the warm lights over the dining room table lending light to the family room.

The large, solid chocolate lab cuddling gently with the fragile looking little girl. Sophie imagined how this scene might be similar to how a family spends evenings together. Not her family. It was strange to think that someone she just met a short time ago allowed strangers into his home. His wife not even questioning and to be so hospitable. Adding to that, two of the guests were taking up unapproved residence in a vacant building. *If someone had asked me a week ago if I thought I would be here, I would have thought them to be crazy. I would have been, should have been, in my new apartment, unpacking, eating take out off paper plates and hanging pictures on my wall, trying to figure out the best placement and shopping for new accessories. I will certainly be unpacking but in a completely unfamiliar place.*

Her thoughts were broken by Jamison finding something of interest in the box. He had a childlike excitement sharing the photos. It was similar to the contagious exuberance that Charlie exhibited while playing with Chili. "Here we go, take a look at these!" Jamison exclaimed.

Sophie stood up and leaned over the table to view the sea of pictures flowing over the hefty coffee table. She took the stack of assorted sizes that Jamison handed her and flipped through them. All old pictures had the same style no matter who was in them. Similar expressions, similar paper, similar backgrounds although in different areas. After a sudden chill in the air, Sophie wandered toward the fireplace as she was thumbing through the photos.

Jamison picked up a large, eleven-by-fourteen-inch print. "Here it is! Here is a picture of the building back in the day. It was a hopping place for many years. Here are a few more," Jamison said as he found a couple of smaller, more manageable prints.

"Check this out. The clothing, the character of the bar. Just what you would expect to see in the 20s," Justin added.

"I can almost hear the music playing in the background and the chatter of the people moving around," Mae said.

"There is something kind of enchanting or inspiring about these," Sophie said.

"I couldn't agree more." Jamison glided over to his wife and held out his hand for her to take it, hinting to get up and dance with him. "Mae I?" he said with a wink.

She obliged him and they glided around the spacious family room a couple times before settling back on the sectional.

"Has Jamison told you about the legend of the Blue Owl?" Mae asked.

"No, he hasn't," Sophie said, raising her eyebrows with interest.

"There were whispers of a legend that haunted the minds of the locals. According to some, the Blue Owl operated as a speakeasy during prohibition. There was a room in the cellar that was used as a gathering area. It was called the Indigo Room. Secluded, in hopes to be kept secret and to be protected from raids. Alcohol was kept in the Indigo room as well as a storage room, underground. There was a long, narrow, dusty hallway with dirt floors and cobblestone walls that led to the Indigo Room. There were strange occurrences documented. These events were witnessed by patrons as well as the staff that worked there," Mae said.

"You could say the spirits there came on many different levels," Jamison added.

"Some of the witnesses claimed they heard noises like the cries of a child. Some could attest to hearing whispers of a little girl. Words you couldn't quite make out. There was a sense of eerie discontent, even tremendous feelings of fear associated with these peculiar events. Patrons were uneasy as they traveled down the long, dimly lit hallway to the secret room. Other witnesses say the door to the Indigo Room would close by itself. A heavy wood door that didn't close easily. These strange occurrences, while creating a sense of supernatural presence had some patrons frightened to return, created intrigue for other patrons and maybe even helped business. This was a popular topic for discussion while spirits were being served, people speculating about the event and circumstances leading up to it," Mae said.

Jamison, digging through the box, pulled out a piece of yellowed paper torn on the left edge as if torn out of a book. "Here is something that may be a journal entry or just a documentation of an event." Handing it to Sophie.

The page was old and fragile, but still intact. There were a couple stains on it near the top corner. The penmanship was very nice. Cursive writing.

"What does it say?" asked Justin.

Sophie read the words on the page aloud.

"'Tonight was no ordinary night. Peculiar things are happening around here. After another busy evening, I was cleaning up in the cellar room, taking the rest of the glasses to the kitchen for washing. The light dimmed and flickered in what we call the Indigo Room. It went out. Completely dark. I stopped, holding the bucket of glasses and couldn't see my hand in front of my face. At first, I thought, Applesauce! What a time for the bulb to go out. That's when a slight cool wind breezed by my face. The back of my neck and arms filled with goosebumps. "Who's there, I called out." I heard a whisper but couldn't make out what was said. Then the lights flickered and came back on. I felt as if I wasn't alone down there, but nobody was around when the lights came back on.'"

"Is it signed?" Justin asked.

"Nope, that's all that's on here. Maybe there was another page?" Sophie said.

The medication Mae gave Sophie for her head wore off and the pain returned to the side of her forehead and combined with the exhaustion of the day. She rubbed her eyes with her hands, trying to rub the tension and exhaustion away too. She was facing the coffee table still full of pictures even more spread out and sorted through. One caught her eye. An eight-by-ten size portrait of a woman. Most of it was covered by the other pictures, but she could see the short, dark, chin-length hair that had been so familiar recently.

She looked a lot like... No, it can't possibly be her! It was! The lady from my dream. A prickly sensation formed on the back of her neck. Her heart skipped a beat. *Who was in this photograph and why was she haunting my sleep? This feels a bit surreal. Being in a strange house, moving out of my apartment, the breakup, all this newness at once. Nothing is familiar except this haunting woman.* The sound of the woman's raspy voice asking, "Did you find the key?" She hoped they didn't notice the turmoil going on inside of her. She didn't want to bring up the dream. Not yet at least until she found out more information. *Get it together. Take a breath.*

"Who is the lady in this photo?" Sophie asked as calmly as she could.

"That lady was one of the Blue Owl owners," Jamison said.

Sophie's head was filled with even more questions. This lady was a real person. *Who is she and why is she visiting my dreams and asking about keys?* It was coincidental that she was an owner of the bar at one time and now Sophie owned it. But what did that mean? Her mind, working overtime, spiraled into more questions that would make her head hurt more if she thought about them tonight.

As much as she tried to hide it, Justin noticed some uneasiness from Sophie. Justin gestured toward the sleeping girl. "It's getting late. We should be going soon. If that's ok with you? Since you are our ride." Looking at Sophie.

She appreciated him seizing the opportunity and initiating the exit.

"Here. Please. Take these pictures. I have so many of them.

Maybe they will bring you some inspiration." Jamison handed her a stack of assorted sized photographs, including the one of the mystery woman.

"Thank you. And thank you both very much for dinner and the company," Sophie said.

After thanking them as well, Justin carefully approached the sleeping girl and lifted her off the couch, trying not to disturb her. Chili let out a sigh with a grumble at the end of it, showing her disappointment that her new friend was leaving. He smiled at the dog and patted her softly on the head. "You'll see her again."

"And Sophie, give some thought to that offer. I am serious about the partnership with restoring the bar," Jamison said.

"I will consider your offer," Sophie said.

Sophie intended on dropping Justin and his daughter off and heading to her hotel. Acting on impulse, she blurted out, "I'm so glad I unloaded the car earlier. I can't wait to get to my hotel room and fall into that big bed." Then regret kicked in, realizing the situation. *Oh geez! What was I thinking? That I was dropping them off at their home? Do I apologize? Or would that make it worse? Good thing it's not a far drive.* She pulled up along the curb in front of the building and shifted the car into park.

"Sorry," Sophie said softly. Not attempting to give any kind of pathetic explanation.

Then she thought of the sweet little girl sleeping on that dirty old mattress in the dark vacant building, just after spending the evening cuddled with Chili on Jamison's cozy couch. She couldn't send them in there without at least offering the hotel as an option. Clean bedding, a shower, and breakfast, at least for now. *He couldn't be that bad, right? I just spent the evening with him. Plus, he did rescue me earlier.*

Justin got out of the passenger side and went to open the back door of the vehicle to carry his daughter in. Sophie rolled down the passenger window to get his attention. He leaned in the window.

"I have plenty of room in my hotel. It's a suite with a bedroom. There is a pull-out bed you could have. Clean sheets for her and breakfast in the morning."

"If it's about what you said, it's not a big deal. Really. You didn't choose this," Justin said.

"No, it's not about that. Just get in," Sophie said.

"I'm too tired to argue and I'm sure she will be grateful for that. I am. Thank you."

"No worries," she said as she motioned her head for him to sit back in the seat he just vacated.

CHAPTER 16

Charlie was slumped over, sound asleep with her waves of golden hair spilling over Justin's shoulder. Sophie made up the pull-out sofa bed for them in the living area of her hotel suite. His well-toned arms held her light frame with ease. Sophie took a few glances but didn't want to stare, making it more awkward than it already was. *What was I thinking inviting strangers into my hotel room?* But there was something endearing about the way he was holding her. Something protective.

Sophie finished up, spreading out the thin cotton hotel blanket over the smooth, bleach-scented white sheets, grabbed a few of her things laying on the coffee table as quickly as she could, and retired to the bedroom for the evening. She quietly closed the door and briefly stood behind it, skeptical of her decision to invite them to stay. There was no going back on it now and it had been a long, exhausting day. Yawning, Sophie made her way over to the bed where her overnight bag was. While carefully digging through her neatly folded, packed clothes looking for something resembling pajamas, she thought how relieved and grateful she was, given the circumstances, that the lady at the front desk upgraded her to a suite. Free of charge as compensation after a mix up with her reservation. The separate bedroom was a nice reprieve.

Alone at last. She could settle in from the events that transpired during the day.

After getting ready and crawling into bed, Sophie switched off the lamp on the nightstand. She closed her eyes, relieved that she could drift off to sleep and get some rest. She had been exhausted a few minutes ago but now found a second wind. Her body was tired, but her brain was wide awake, replaying conversations and information at warp speed. Jamison had offered an option to consider, during the discussion at dinner. Now her mind was filled with thoughts and possibilities to consider about the bar, the storefront, and the apartments. She clicked the light back on and sat up against the large wood headboard, propping the pillows up behind her. At first, her objective was to sell the building and move on, but now things were different.

New information came in that she had to consider. Most importantly, she needed somewhere to live. Keeping one of the apartment units would solve that problem. Next, she needed income. Since she couldn't renew her old job and the new counseling position fell through, she needed to apply for other positions or figure out another option. Selling would bring a lump sum in right away which would be helpful, but she could not ignore the opportunity for long term income. The downside was the time and money it would take to get it renovated and up and running. Jamison mentioned he had the funding for renovations if she took him on as a partner.

The store space could be rented out, as well as the second apartment unit. She thought of the two strangers in the next room. Maybe they would be interested in the second apartment unit. If she hired Justin, they would be able to pay rent. Or work something out in trade at least until the business was fully operational. If there was a way Sophie could help that little girl find a home and help provide some type of solution, it was worth a try.

With all the ideas and questions flooding her brain, she needed to put them on paper for visual effect. The pen and notepad in the drawer on the nightstand would do. She jotted some notes down and doodles in between spurts of ideas. She listed questions that would need answering. Licensing, purchasing, renovations, permits, financing, accounting, software, business classes, resources, menu, staff, furniture, marketing. The list went on. She was on a roll. Finally, after about an hour, she was tired enough to put the notepad down and fall asleep.

After the guests had left for the evening, Mae asked Jamison if he took the skeleton key out of the box since he did not mention it was in his possession while their dinner guests were perusing through old photos. He carefully pulled it out of his pocket, displaying it for her as if it was a sacred artifact.

"Why didn't you give that to Sophie? If it's a key to her building..." Mae said, but before she could finish, Jamison interjected.

"I need to search that cellar, Mae. It's the final piece of the puzzle. Or at least a step closer to solving it."

"Are you sure there is even anything there? After all this time?" Mae asked.

"There has to be. For so many years my family has been consumed with finding out the truth. My father's life was spent collecting information and stories surrounding that time. The agony of knowing there was more to the story. More than anyone would tell. The best kept secret of the century, at least in our lives. He suffered the agony of not knowing for so long. All the years of speculation eating away. Guessing and wondering if others knew and judged him or our family. It wore away at him and I can't have the same wear away at me. Not knowing is the worst part and not knowing who to trust. If I can just search that cellar, I may be able to find a clue to shed some light on things. Or if there is something of value hidden. Either way, we need to find it," said Jamison.

"Are you sure offering to get involved in a partnership is the right thing?" Mae asked.

"It's the only way to get close enough to search and have access to the property without causing suspicion. I don't know how much she knows about the history," Jamison said.

"From the discussion tonight, it appears that she doesn't know much about it," Mae said.

"Maybe, but there was one moment after looking at the photographs, I got a sense that she knows more than she let on," Jamison said. "I'd like to keep it under wraps for the moment. At least until I can get in there and take a look around. It's hard to know who to trust. If she knows about my family, our history or what could be in that building that she now owns, there is no telling what could happen," Jamison said with concern.

"She has no connection to any of this. Just that she was given a property by an old patient of hers that took comfort in her care and wanted to give whatever he had to her after passing," Mae said.

"Since we can't be sure and know very little about her, we need to keep this quiet for a while. I have the only access key to that cellar. I will just happen to find the key lying around. There is so much stuff in there, it's plausible for a key to get misplaced and not easily spotted. This is the only way I can see that will work," Jamison said.

"Do you even know what you're looking for?" Mae asked.

"The stories from family members and friends of my father, along with the notes he left, point to something that is hidden or a clue to find something somewhere in the cellar of the old Blue Owl. I'm not certain of what it is, but I believe I will know it when I see it. There are two rooms and a long hallway down there. It can't take long to search," Jamison said.

"Be careful. You may find more than you are looking for. More than you want to know. Just be sure that is the door you want to open," Mae added.

CHAPTER 17

The morning sun shone through the small gap between two sheer window curtain panels in the hotel bedroom. As Sophie pulled up the fluffy, white down comforter, there was something weighing on it in the bed next to her. She glanced over to find a small figure with an abundance of curly hair asleep next to her. She tried to move the covers carefully, but Charlie started to stir from the movement. Charlie opened her big, bright blue eyes and gave Sophie a smile from ear to ear. It made Sophie's heart smile. At that moment she realized, she would probably do anything for that little girl. Even though they had just met a few days ago and had spent a short time together, Sophie was glad she got to stay in a warm place with clean bedding.

"Goooood morning, sunshine. How did you sleep?" Sophie asked.

"Great! But my Daddy was gone. I couldn't find him, so I came in here. Is that okay?"

Sophie smiled at her warmly, "Yes, it's fine. Are you hungry?"

She nodded her head yes. Sophie got out of bed, opened the bedroom door, and slowly peeked out to check on her other guest. Justin was sleeping on the pullout bed. After making herself somewhat presentable for the hotel lobby, Sophie and Charlie explored the breakfast buffet. They brought an assortment of bagels, muffins, donuts, and eggs back to the room for Justin. He was awake, had the bed put away, blankets neatly folded resting on one end of the sofa and was sitting on the opposite end by the time they got back to the room.

"I was just wondering where you ran off to," Justin said, smiling at Charlie as she ran over to jump up in his lap. She wrapped her little delicate arms around his neck.

"I could ask you the same thing," Sophie said under her breath. "Breakfast?" This time with a slightly louder tone, holding up the plate. "We ran down to the lobby. You were sleeping. I didn't want to disturb you."

"I figured it was something like that, unless it was aliens that came to take you back to their planet of the dogs," he said playfully, picking her up over his shoulder as he stood up, Charlie giggling.

"We brought you some food, Daddy."

"Alien. Must. Eat. Chicken leg?" Reaching for her leg and pretending to bite.

He lowered her safely to the ground and asked what she found. She carefully carried the plate of food over to him. He offered her something off the plate first.

"Thanks, but I already ate downstairs with Sophie."

"Alright, more for me then," Justin said.

Charlie ran off to the bathroom after two cups of apple juice and a little bit of milk that she drank downstairs. Maybe that was too much to drink for a little girl; Sophie wasn't sure, but she knew she wasn't going to stop her from eating or drinking since there was no telling when she would eat next. Standing with folded arms at first, she moved to a chair to sit while Justin was eating the muffin from the plate of food.

"Thank you again for letting us stay here, and for breakfast. We will get out of your hair shortly. I'm sure you have things to do," Justin said.

Before she had time to respond, the little girl ran up to her side, leaned in, and whispered in Sophie's ear.

"Can I swim in the pool in there?" Charlie asked pointing to the bathroom.

Sophie laughed out loud. She thought it was adorable, but to a small child that Jacuzzi tub in the bathroom probably was as big as a pool.

"Of course, you can. I mean if it's okay with your Daddy and if you can stay for a little while longer," Sophie said.

Charlie had a world of fun in that "pool." Sophie was amazed at the mind of a child and the excitement over every little thing. It could have just been Charlie's unique personality. A gift to see the good. Either way, she thought if she ever had a daughter, she hoped she would be like Charlie.

They finished getting ready and the little girl came galloping out to the living area wearing the new outfit Sophie bought her at the gift shop on their way to get breakfast. The outfit consisted of colorful printed leggings with various lines and stripes of teal blue, lime green, pink, and purple and a coordinating teal blue shirt with a butterfly in the middle filled with the same pattern as the leggings.

"Like my new outfit?" Charlie asked proudly.

"Wow! Very lovely. Yes. I do like it," Justin said.

He appeared so attentive to her. Did he really leave the hotel last night? Was she mistaken when she said he wasn't there? Sophie couldn't bear the thought of sending them off to who knows where in this cold weather. There had to be another solution. Given her own recent change in circumstances, she had a new appreciation for their situation. Why did he keep leaving her alone like the first day they met? Where was he going? She knew it really wasn't any of her business, but she was determined to find out anyway.

CHAPTER 18

Since making the decision to live in one of the upstairs apartment units of her newly acquired building, she wanted to get
a jump on cleaning and preparing it so she could check out of
the hotel. The sooner, the better. When Justin, Charlie, and
Sophie arrived together, Justin volunteered to help with the
cleaning or any repairs needed to express his appreciation for
everything she had done for him and his daughter.

As soon as the three of them crossed the side street from
the parking lot, Sophie handed Justin the key to unlock the
building. She realized she left something in the car and turned
around to head back. Upon returning to her vehicle, something caught her attention in the driver's side window. A jolt
of recognition spiked through her as she saw a flash of a
woman's face in the reflection. There she was again! The
woman from her dream which had become more of a nightmare. It took Sophie's breath away for a second as a small
heart palpitation caught her off guard. The air was still for a
moment and then a light, cool breeze brushed by her. Sophie
felt it blow almost through her as she heard her name. Not a
whisper but someone calling it out. "Sophie." She turned her
head and looked up toward the building. Nothing. She turned
to look in the opposite direction. Nothing.

"Well, that was freaky," Sophie said as she entered the

building, catching up with the other two.

"What is it?" Justin asked.

"Did you hear something outside just a minute ago?"

"Just me unlocking the door," Justin said.

"Hmm." Sophie looked back outside the door and down the street. All was quiet.

"All good?"

"Yeah, yeah, everything is fine." Sophie shook it off and did not want to even bring up the image she had seen in the window reflection.

She welcomed the distraction of Charlie's endless energy, overflowing with excitement to get started on her new under the sea coloring book. Charlie asked if she could open her new crayons and spread them out to see all the colors. Justin cleared an area, moving miscellaneous items to a table while Sophie got a rag and some cleaner to wipe down a space for her to work. The little girl climbed up with ease onto the stool. She was stronger than her little frame looked. Without hesitation, she made her way into the box of crayons and stretched out the twenty-four colors, looking for her first choice.

Sophie dipped the rag in the warm soapy water and wrung out the excess water. Justin turned toward her. "Thank you for the things you bought for her. You have been more than generous with everything. Please don't think that we expect that from you. But it is appreciated. More than you know."

"You're very welcome. She is a sweet girl," Sophie said. *She deserves the world.*

"I have been looking for a place for us." Justin paused. "It's complicated. It's just taking more time than I hoped, but anyway we will be out by the day we agreed upon," Justin said.

"Actually, I wanted to talk to you about that. I was up most of the night thinking about what Jamison suggested. At first his idea seemed ridiculous and out of reach. Something I never would have considered. It's just not in my wheelhouse. But I'm learning that sometimes you have to adapt to change," Sophie said.

"I can definitely understand that," Justin said.

"Allowing myself to look at it a little more closely, keeping the building could solve a few problems. I have no place to go. So, I can understand a little of your situation. I realize circumstances are different, but I get it. So, holding onto the building and living in one of the apartment units is the best solution for me. There are two apartments. I wanted to offer the other one to you and your daughter," Sophie said.

"Thank you for the offer, but I'm not sure I can do that," Justin said.

"If it's about the money, I am thinking about taking Jamison up on his partnership offer. I could renovate and re-open the business. That means I need to hire security among other positions. If you're interested, the job is yours. You passed the interview with flying colors. But since I wouldn't be able to pay you right away, at least until things were up and running, maybe we can work something out with housing," Sophie said.

"Our situation is complicated. But I will certainly help out for as long as I can," Justin said.

Sophie was tempted to inquire about the complications and bring up his disappearing act but decided against it. It was none of her business and she was trying to offer a place to stay and a job, not scare him off. She decided to hold off until another time. If there was one.

"Okay, well the offer stands. Just let me know." She smiled warmly at him.

Sophie scooped up her keys off the counter and asked Charlie if she wanted to go exploring with them. Of course, she was up for the adventure. They walked outside the building to the right and into the alcove next to the storefront just a few paces from the entrance. They entered a doorway to a secluded set of stairs leading up to the second-floor apartment units. At the top of the scuffed stairway, surrounded by dingy old walls, there was a door to the left and a door to the right. Sophie unlocked both paint chipped and smudged white doors. They entered the door to the right.

The first thing that hit their noses as they entered was the warm, musty smell from being closed up for many years. There were a few items of furniture, an old dresser, end tables, and a coffee table, covered with dust-colored canvas cloths. The hardwood floors needed some attention but were mostly in good shape. The space was larger than expected from the outside view between the higher ceilings, the large picture window toward the front, and the open layout of the kitchen, dining area, and living space with no borders. The living area was up front toward the window. The kitchen bordered the wall to the left. It had a good size island separating it from the dining area. Sophie pictured people gathered around the island, engaged in conversation and laughter. It was a two-bedroom, one bath unit. The bedrooms and bath were down the hall, opposite the kitchen, dining, and living area. There was a four-foot entryway, covered with hardwood flooring; decent condition with a few worn spots. Just beyond the entry, there was a wall, directing left, down the hall toward the bedrooms and bath or right, toward the living area.

Sophie was pleasantly surprised at how large the bedrooms were. The bathroom had 1950s style, small black and white tile. There was definitely a vintage charm to the apartment that Sophie could appreciate. It certainly wasn't brand new, but the condition was decent and she could work with it. It was hers. At that moment, the recently unknown was starting to take shape into a new opportunity which sparked both pride and excitement. There were many possibilities of what she could make it into. As they were walking around, she could start to envision arranging furniture, her choice of color palette, her stuff around the apartment. It needed cleaning more than anything else. A few minor repairs and it needed to have some junk removed but in good shape for the most part. Sophie could see past the surface to imagine what could be. Considering she still had the better part of the day to work on it, the possibility to make a good size dent and be able to move in the next day or so was motivation for her to get started.

The three of them ventured to the second apartment unit. It was empty with the exception of a slight echo. There was nothing to clear out. The layout was a mirror image of the first apartment. They walked into the same musty smell, so they opened the windows to let the breeze breathe life back into the space. It was a sunny, fall day with a crisp breeze but comfortable temperature. Most of the rooms needed a coat of fresh paint to liven them up. The floors were in better condition than the first unit. Cleaning was also top on the list. In her mind, Sophie was running down the list of things to do. She could uncover the furniture, haul out any junk, and stop by the store to pick up more cleaning supplies, paint, and any other necessary items.

Justin made his way to the kitchen to test the water just as he did in the other unit. The kitchen faucet sprung a leak as soon as the water turned on, spraying his face and shirt, soaking the front of him. He immediately reached for the lever to shut it off. Sophie's mental to-do list was cut short. He pulled up the end of his already wet t-shirt and wiped his face, exposing the waistband of his jeans, the top edge of his navy boxer shorts, and above that, surprisingly pleasant, well-defined abs under smooth white skin. She couldn't help but look and who could blame her. She quickly turned away, but not before he caught her wandering eye.

"How are you at plumbing?" Sophie blurted out trying to avoid the embarrassment. Then realizing that may not have been a good avenue for the conversation either.

"I know my way around a sink," Justin said.

"There has to be some tools around this place somewhere. Maybe back downstairs," Sophie said.

"I'll check it out and I need a new shirt," Justin said as they made their way back downstairs to the other part of the property.

Sophie passed by the cellar door and tried opening the handle, thinking there would be something of use down there in storage, but it was locked. She searched around for the key but had no luck. "Find anything in there?" she asked Justin who had gone to search the kitchen and storage area.

"Found it," he said a couple of seconds later.

There was a small toolbox on a shelf in the kitchen. Justin set it down on one of the tables near the door to the storefront. He entered the room that was his temporary home and picked up a clean white t-shirt from the chair it was hanging over. He was shirtless for a few seconds, heading back toward the area where Sophie was, putting the clean shirt on while walking, exposing an entire upper body as toned as the abs. Also revealing a large scar on his shoulder. Sophie was curious what would have happened to cause the scar. Not wanting to get caught a second time, she turned away and busied herself looking for her purse and keys.

She needed to get out for a while. She needed to give Delia Parker and Jamison a call to let them know her new objective regarding the property. First, she needed to stop at the city offices to take care of some paperwork for the building.

"I'll be back in a bit. I'm going to run some errands. Is there anything you need for the sink?" Sophie asked.

"Good for now, but I'll let you know if we need to kayak our way out of here." Justin said.

"Use the Force," Sophie said.

On the way out, Charlie showed Sophie the picture of the tropical fish she was working so hard on using every color in her crayon box. Sophie gave a thumbs up and her high five approval then headed out the door.

CHAPTER 19

The city offices were only a few miles from her new home. She sat in the car before going in, to make a couple phone calls. The first was to Delia Parker since there was no need to keep the appointment later that day in light of her decision. She informed Delia of the new direction she was taking with the property and thanked her for all her help. Delia wished her luck with her new endeavor and asked Sophie to remember her and extend an invitation to the grand opening.

Her next call was to Jamison Brooks. She paused before calling to make sure taking this leap was what she wanted to do. *Just jump in. Count to three, jump on two, right?* She pressed the call button. He was very happy to hear that Sophie had accepted his partnership offer. They agreed to meet very soon to go over an estimate of costs and timeline for the renovations. He was more than willing to clear his schedule to take a look around and assess what needed to be done. After she ended the phone call, she took the next step and entered the city offices to submit the necessary paperwork for her new building.

Sophie found the building department on the upper level of the city office. She made her way to the line at the counter. There were two people ahead of her. A woman in front of her wore a dark business suit with low heels. The man ahead of the lady in the business suit was dressed in a dark gray hoodie with white paint smudges, including one near the construction company logo on the front. He wore white painter's pants with a variety of colors smudged on them. His well-used work boots had an equal amount of paint and other stains. While she was waiting, Sophie glanced around at all the directional signs of what line to enter depending on the purpose or paperwork. She was hoping she was in the right place to drop off the form the attorney gave her to submit. She would find out soon enough.

They waited in line a few minutes and the clerk approached the counter and called the man wearing the paint smudges up for service. After explaining what he needed, the clerk walked away to an office and came back minutes later. The painter shifted his weight back and forth during an extended wait time. His hands went from on the counter to his pockets, then eventually he folded his arms, exerting slight irritation with the wait time. He turned to the two ladies behind him and shook his head. He let out a sigh expressing his building frustration. When the clerk returned, the man was not happy with what she had to say. The man had some heated questions and words of dissatisfaction. Then he slammed the paper in his hand down on the counter. He gained the attention of the few people in the vicinity, including Sophie.

"This is the third time this has happened! There is no reason for it! What is going on here? I want to talk to him," the man said with frustration rising inside him.

"I'm sorry, sir, but he's in a meeting," the clerk said.

"You just came from his office; He's not in a meeting," the man said in disbelief. "This is ridiculous!"

"Uh, he's unavailable at the moment, sir."

"He's hiding in his office is what he's doing because he knows it's not right," the man said.

"I'm sorry, sir. You can leave your number and I can have

someone give you a call," the clerk offered.

The man shook his head in disgust and turned to walk away. "Yeah, I'm sure they will get right on that," the man said as he walked away in a huff.

There was a tension in the air after that exchange. The clerk brushed it off and blamed the display on hot-headed contractors. She was not very friendly or personable as Sophie approached the counter when it was her turn. In her peripheral vision, Sophie noticed a man in a dress shirt and tie on a cell phone peeking out of the city manager's office. He hesitated while scanning the area then proceeded to walk out and down the hall. Luckily Sophie had a quick and easy task of turning in a form. The clerk took the form, stamped it, and sent her on her way.

As Sophie entered the center revolving door to exit the building, she could see two men about ten feet away on the other side having a discussion. The exaggerated hand movements from the man wearing the shirt and tie that Sophie saw duck out of his office a few minutes ago caught her attention. The other man looked slightly familiar, but she could not place him. Then just as she was going to step out of the doorway, she realized he looked like one of the men that tried to attack her. At the last second, she pivoted into the doorway, continuing back into the building, safe from view. She ducked over to the side out of the way of the occasional traffic in and out of the building to get a better view of the men without being seen. She had a good view through the glass from the other doors and windows. Her eyes fixed on them with laser focus. The man in the shirt and tie turned toward the building after a few more seconds. Sophie thought for sure he was looking at her and that she had somehow drawn attention or they knew she was watching. He headed toward the door straight for her. *He couldn't have seen me, could he?* She quickly turned her back to the door and pretended to dig around in her purse for something.

"Excuse me, ma'am." Sophie thought she was discovered. She looked up from her purse and raised her eyebrows in that "can I help you?" manner. The man in the shirt and tie was staring straight into her eyes. He nodded at something past her. Her pulse quickened, and a warmth rose in her body all the way to her cheeks as she turned her head. She then saw the circle button for the elevator just on the other side of her that she was blocking.

Processing so many questions in her mind along with fear and anger all in seconds. *Who was the guy he was talking* to? *How are they connected?* Maintaining her composure, "Oh, yes, of course, sorry." She smiled at the man politely and escaped out of the building with relief.

CHAPTER 20

Attempting to switch gears, Sophie channeled her energy into something more productive. It was time to focus on the task in front of her, which consisted of prepping and cleaning the apartments. First, she removed all the dust cloths to reveal furniture to be sorted through. Second, she took a mental inventory of items to keep and items to eliminate. Third, Justin assisted her with moving the usable furniture in place. There were a few extra pieces that had a vintage charm Sophie didn't want to part with. Justin suggested holding them until they had a chance to refinish them. They hauled the leftover junk out to the dumpster behind the building. Lastly, they cleaned and scrubbed the bathrooms, kitchens, floors, and walls including the beautiful, thick, white base molding.

Making one last round with the broom, Sophie wanted to clear the cobwebs out of the nook toward the back of the apartment. There was a section of the wood flooring that looked different. It didn't quite match. She shined her cell phone flashlight on the floor in the dark corner. There was a four-by-four section of the floor that had a sliding lock on one end. Sophie kneeled on the floor to get a closer look. It was some sort of door. She reached the lock and slid it open. It stuck at first. Issuing a little more force, it unlocked. She pulled the door up and it rested comfortably on the wall. There was a makeshift string with a hook on the wall and a loop on the inside of the door to hold it open. She shined her light down the hole. There was a narrow, rickety-looking ladder. She wanted to find out where it went. She carefully and lightly inserted her leg into the opening, found the first step of the ladder, and settled her foot on it. With a good grip on the floor, she pressed her foot down harder to make sure the ladder wouldn't move under her weight. Sounding sturdy enough, she trustingly lowered her other leg and descended a little further into the opening. Shining her light in the area, she saw some of the kitchen supplies and what looked like the kitchen storage room. She carefully climbed down the next several steps and found solid ground. The door had connected a secret path from her apartment to the corner of the kitchen storage room. She yelled up the ladder through the opening.

"Hey, come check this out!"

Justin went over to the nook where the trap door was open. He carefully climbed through the opening and down the ladder, meeting Sophie at the bottom. The placement of the kitchen storage shelving and debris made for a tight space at the bottom of the ladder. They were face to face and Justin caught a scent of Sophie's perfume. He paused in the moment, noticing her hair pulled up in a clip; the wisps of hair lightly falling from each side landed gently on her exposed neck.

"Cool, huh?" Sophie asked.

"Very! I wonder what it was for. Must have been some purpose," Justin said.

"I was just thinking about that. I bet they used it for the cash. Move it from the bar to a secret place. Maybe they had a safe. There is plenty of space in that nook to hold one. Inconspicuous spot," Sophie said.

"Yes, that would make sense. Move it so nobody sees it. Nice!" Justin added.

They made their way through the maze of storage items

and into the kitchen. Justin stopped at the sink to show Sophie how the plumbing was working again in the kitchen as well as in both apartments. Luckily, the hardware store just across the street made running out for parts a couple times very convenient. Charlie was in the next room, entertained with watching a movie on Sophie's tablet. The novelty of technology that she wasn't used to having. Charlie called out to Sophie to let her know her phone was ringing. Sophie caught it just in time to see it was Grayce Reed. Sophie was expecting her call. Grayce was in the area and wanted to stop in and see her.

"Hi Grayce, did you find the building okay?"

"This place is hopping, love! I'll be inside in just a minute. It took a bit to find parking. There is some sort of community event going on. All the lots are full and a herd of people making their way down the street," Grayce said.

"I'll meet you at the door," Sophie said.

When Sophie opened the doors, she could hear faint music from around the block. Several people were walking down the block toward the direction of the music. Some carrying coolers, blankets, chairs; the street was lined with cars in every available spot. The lot next to her building was crammed with parked cars. Grayce walked up to greet Sophie. Charlie and Justin had just stepped out the door to see what all the activity was about.

"Someone mentioned they are having music in the park around the corner tonight. Activities for kids too, I hear. Could be a fun evening," Grayce said as she smiled at Charlie.

"A change of scenery might be nice," Sophie said.

"Would you like to join us?" Justin asked.

"Thank you for the offer, love. Another time? Harlan made reservations for dinner tonight. I won't keep you long. I was just in the area, and I wanted to stop in and thank you again, for everything," Grayce said.

"Not necessary at all. It was my pleasure," Sophie said.

"If there is ever anything I can do, please don't hesitate to ask, okay?" Grayce said.

"I will keep that in mind. Thank you. Since you're here would you like a tour?"

"I have been looking forward to it. I bet it will be quite a transformation," Grayce said.

CHAPTER 21

Charlie was immediately drawn to the playground, with wide eyes focused on its large, colorful play structure including a slide and fort-like area with a variety of levels. Justin found a vacant spot on the cement half wall near the play area. Of course, Charlie's first question was asking to go play, but not before a vendor came around with popcorn. The vendor, a young twenty-something, dressed very trendy, also sported a bright pink, gourmet popcorn company hoodie. Nice and thick for a fall evening. His freshly styled, moderately long hair held a section of hot pink highlights that complemented his hoodie. He was holding a black and white striped box with hot pink writing in one arm and a neatly packed, clear cellophane package, sealed and tied with a matching hot pink ribbon. The bag was filled with popcorn in colorfully coated pastels.

"Free cotton candy flavored popcorn? If it's okay with your mom," he said, looking from Charlie to Sophie.

"Oh, I'm not her mom, but I think her Dad would be alright with it. Thank you," Sophie said, glancing at Justin for approval on the popcorn.

"It's fine." Justin nodded as the vendor handed Sophie the bag of popcorn.

"Can I try a piece?" Charlie asked. Sophie untied the ribbon, opened the bag, and handed Charlie a few pieces. A rush of cherry, strawberry, blue raspberry, green apple, and a hint of vanilla enticed their senses.

Sophie turned to Justin and gave him a handful of the colored pieces, several stuck together from the sugary glaze. "Does she see her mother?" There was some hesitation answering the question. Justin shifted his eyes toward Charlie, which suggested it may not be an appropriate time to discuss it. Sophie took the hint and did not press.

"Which color is your favorite?" Sophie asked.

"I like them all!" Charlie was distracted by the activity from the play area. Swings in motion, kids on the twirly slide, climbers on the colorful dome structure. She could barely contain the energy from running over there.

"Go ahead," Justin said, nodding in the direction of the playground that was just a few feet away. He barely got the words out and she was darting over to the play structure. Justin and Sophie took a seat on the cement half wall.

"Sorry about before. I didn't mean to pry," Sophie said.

"No, it's fine. Complicated situation. There's not an easy answer that makes sense. You know, like we are separated, or she passed away. Too long of a story to get into here." Justin looked around at the people passing by while the sultry sound of a guitar played blues music in the background. "But the short version is that I returned from deployment about a month ago to a home that was very different from when I left it. It wasn't safe for Charlie. So here we are," Justin said.

"But why not stay in a hotel or rent an apartment?" Sophie asked.

"Like I said, it's complicated," Justin said.

"I just mean that it must have been bad if a vacant building was the safer choice," Sophie said. She could judge by his shifting on the wall, his hesitation in the discussion and sudden folding of his arms that he was quickly becoming uncomfortable with the topic. The conversation was cut short by Charlie running up and hopping on the wall, looking for more popcorn.

Sophie was curious to know what the story was. Justin did not fit the picture of what she imagined a homeless man would look like. Not that there was a one size fits all look to homelessness; after all, she was technically homeless for a brief period. Still, the evidence showed otherwise. He was well-groomed and so was his daughter. Other than living in a vacant building, she was well taken care of. There was the fact that he disappeared a couple of times and left her alone. She wondered what the complication of their situation was. If she pressed anymore, she wasn't sure what she would be getting into. Plus, did she really want any more complications in her own life? As difficult as it was to get away from the questions swirling around in her mind, she decided to let it go, keep things light for the rest of the evening, and accept that it wasn't any of her business. She didn't want to ruin a fun event.

The climate during the rest of the evening was chilly. Between the cool fall weather as the sun went down and Justin's distracted demeanor, Sophie was doing her best to focus on Charlie discussing the playground, the popcorn, and collecting a few interesting rocks. Justin's words were far and few between. Sophie took that as a hint that heading back would be best. As they approached the building, Charlie asked if she could finish watching her movie on Sophie's tablet. This gave Sophie an opportunity to talk to Justin outside, away from little ears.

"I didn't mean anything by what I said at the park. I'm sure you are doing what you can to take care of her," Sophie said.

"The thing is you don't know us. You don't know our past. You just know that we were trespassing in your building," Justin said.

"Then tell me," Sophie said gently.

Justin shook his head and hesitated before saying anything

more, as if trying to talk himself out of revealing sensitive information to someone he just met and to avoid the raw emotional journey he was about to embark on. He never had anyone to talk about this with until now. He looked back at Sophie and saw her patiently waiting with genuine interest. The soft, concerned expression on her face and something in her eyes instinctively revealed he could trust her with anything.

A sudden and unexpected calm came over him and he began, "When I came home after missing three years of her life, I wanted to make it official, getting married to her mother. But the war zone I came home to was worse than the one I left. The house was run down. Most of the items in the house, including furniture, sold for drugs. Strangers were in and out of the house for days, weeks probably. A pile of blankets on the floor in a dark corner was where she slept. I found her hiding in a cupboard when I came home. She had the same outfit on for days, maybe longer, and who knows what she had been eating. There was hardly any food in the house except a jar of peanut butter. So, we left. The strange thing was that nobody even noticed. Her mother was high and shacked up in the bedroom."

"I'm so sorry. I can't even imagine that," Sophie said.

"It tore me apart seeing her like that. Knowing the condition she was living in and I wasn't there. So, yes, this vacant building felt like the safest choice," Justin said.

"Don't you have family or a friend to stay with?" Sophie asked.

"I have a friend that owns the auto shop around the corner. He has a small living space at the shop. He offered it to us but it's too dangerous with all the equipment and tools. We use his shower and laundry," Justin said.

"Why didn't you stay in a hotel or rent some place?" Sophie asked.

"Worried that she would come looking for us. Looking for Charlie. I didn't want to take the chance of having anything in my name show up where she could find us. I can't take a chance on having her go back to that hell hole. I wanted to lay low for a bit to figure everything out and I didn't have any place to go so it was the best option just for a short time. My friend that owns the auto shop mentioned that this building had been vacant for a while, so I figured that nobody would bother us here. Then ownership changed, and you found us before I had a chance to figure out our next move," Justin said.

Sophie paused, processing everything he unloaded. Overwhelmed for Justin and Charlie in their situation, she looked for an outlet from the emotional weight of the information. She stepped across the cobblestone sidewalk a couple feet to the black lamppost and leaned against the base of it for support.

"Whatever you need, I'll help you anyway I can. There must be something you can do. Contact an attorney?" Sophie said.

"Thank you. It's kind that you take such an interest in Charlie's well-being for someone that we just met, especially considering the circumstances and how we met," Justin said.

"Honestly, I thought this was bad enough. I don't want to even imagine..."

"It's not as bad as you think. Clearly, it's not ideal and I wouldn't recommend it long term, but we've made it work so far," Justin said.

"How?" Sophie asked.

"More of a mindset. Something I had to learn and get good at, being in the military. You can create good or bad in your mind with anything," Justin said. "Just have to adapt to the change."

"I can definitely understand change. I have had quite a few recent changes to my original path. Sort of scary not having one now. I've always had a plan and lists to check things off," Sophie said.

"But you don't have to know every detail right now. Isn't there some freedom with not knowing?" Justin asked.

"Yeah, I guess there is. I never thought of it like that. Like there are more possibilities. Nothing written in stone." Sophie said.

"Too rigid of a plan takes away the fun. Part of the journey are the clues revealed along the way," Justin said.

"And I'm the one that is supposed to be the psychologist here," Sophie said.

"What? You mean a psychologist who doesn't know everything?" Justin said playfully.

As they walked back inside, Sophie mentioned she was heading back to the hotel soon. She was eagerly anticipating sitting in the hot tub and then doing some online shopping in her pajamas and a fluffy down comforter.

"Can we stay with you at the hotel again?" Charlie asked.

"Of course, you can," Sophie said.

"Actually, I have to go do something. Would you take her there and I will catch up later?" Justin asked.

"Sure," Sophie said hesitatingly.

When Sophie and Charlie arrived at the hotel, Sophie mentioned the big pool the hotel had. Charlie was bright eyed as they passed it and peered through the glass at the aqua blue water in the large rectangle. Sophie had an idea. They stopped in the gift shop which just happened to have a swimsuit Charlie's size. Ready for some swimming, they followed the familiar scent of chlorine that got stronger as they entered the pool area. They splashed around in the pool first. Sophie introduced Charlie to the water with a few simple techniques. A quick dip in the hot tub was a perfect way to finish off the evening, the warm water aiding Sophie's tired muscles from cleaning and moving furniture.

When they returned to the room, Justin was not back yet. Sophie wondered where he went, and the thought of him leaving Charlie alone the few times that she knew of concerned her. Sophie couldn't help speculating possibilities of where he would have gone. Not wanting to be caught off guard again like with Logan, she wanted to be aware of the signs in front of her. Thinking in circles would not help right now. She reminded herself of three things. One, she really didn't know him very well. Two, speculating wouldn't help. Three, she would confront him when he returned.

It was time to shop. Sophie opened her laptop and found a spot on the bed under the fluffy comforter and perused the internet for items still needed for the apartment units. She searched mattresses, bedding, bath accessories, and kitchenware. Charlie joined in the search after inquiring what Sophie was working on. Sophie introduced her to the world of online shopping. Charlie was interested in all the colorful images. They found a bright comforter with a hot pink background and white daisies with a matching sheet set which they added to the cart.

A couple hours and a few hundred dollars later, she received a text from Jamison asking if she was interested in some furniture that a friend of his was getting rid of. He mentioned that his friend was remodeling his basement and had a leather couch and loveseat. She could use all the furniture she could get in order to furnish the two apartment units. Jamison offered to bring it by the next day. Sophie was pleased at how helpful Jamison was with everything.

Still no sign of Justin after a few hours. Sophie was exhausted and was glad she gave him the extra key to get in. Charlie fell asleep about an hour into the shopping extravaganza. She was relieved that the little girl wasn't sitting in the vacant building by herself while he was out. *Where could he have gone and why didn't he say anything? Was he looking for work or hanging out at a bar? Gambling? It's none of my business.* Then she thought of the situation Justin removed the little girl from. Maybe this was the better option. She had to give him the benefit of the doubt. Everything was still so strange. It was like she was living someone else's life. Every aspect of her life was so different from what it was a week ago including the people, her environment, even her career. Right now, Sophie needed to sleep so she could have the energy to deal with her own uncertain future. She had to figure out how to take on a huge renovation project, work with a new partner that she had just met and run a business that she knew nothing about.

CHAPTER 22

Clipboard in hand, Sophie was assessing the needed repairs in the ladies' room, from a fresh coat of paint to replacing tile and fixtures. It wasn't until now that she really noticed the detail of the oversized mirror above the two sinks. The style was more ornate than her taste, almost gaudy, but it had an enchanting quality to it. The thick gold frame around it was sturdy despite its paint chips and worn spots along the shapes and curves, showing its years. The curves of the frame reached up to the top center of the frame, leading to a figurehead of a woman with long, flowing gold hair. It reminded Sophie of something decorative on the bow of a boat, protecting its crew but drawing you in with its beauty and grace. Sophie shifted her eyes downward to the reflection in front of her. The image disappeared as the lights suddenly flickered off and then back on. There was a strange energy in the room, very different from a moment ago. With a sudden pressure on her shoulders and chest, it was as if she was not alone in the room anymore. Recognizing the strange force, she moved quickly toward the door. She remembered the recent discussion at Jamison's dinner party on the hauntings of the Blue Owl. She thought about the strange noises and other reports by people in the building. *It's probably nothing, just old lighting.* She added that to her checklist. *Fix lighting in bathroom.* It wasn't until she reached for the door to open it that the memory flashed in her mind. The figure at the top of the mirror. She had seen that before.

Sophie was eight years old. She remembered looking in that same mirror and staring up at the long haired, golden woman fixed to the top, watching over the women that pass through the door. The memory of visiting this very establishment with her mother was so clear. It was in the middle of the day, during the summer. She remembered how hot it was outside and how cool it was when they entered the building. She remembered wearing her favorite purple athletic shorts with white piping. The building was quiet except for a few people setting up for the evening. She remembered how empty it was, expecting more people to be there. Her mother knew the manager and had to stop by to see her for something.

Sophie remembered the music went on and off like there was some intermittent short issue with the wiring or equipment. When she came out of the bathroom, the music was low enough that she could hear talking from an open door that went down to the lower level. She was curious to see what or who was down there. She peeked around the door. The stairway was dimly lit with a light at the top and at the bottom. The flutter in her stomach was caused by both nerves and excitement. She knew she probably wasn't supposed to be down there. It was unfamiliar territory, but her curiosity won out and she slowly crept, making her way down the stone stairway. The tightly packed dirt walls in some areas, along with the dusty, narrow stairway reminded her of what it would be like heading into a cave. Cautiously lingering at the bottom of the stairs, she could see two men coming out of a room at the end of the hallway. The second man locked the door behind him, and they walked down the hall toward her. She wanted to run up the stairs but couldn't move. She pressed her back to the dirt wall, hiding in the shadow of the stairway as they passed in front of her. They entered another room just a few feet away from her. When the men were out of sight, she quickly approached the door to the first room they came from. The old skeleton key, still in the door, was unlike anything she had seen, with its worn brass color and its three large, artful curves. It was thicker than any key she had seen and it looked solid. She slowly put her hand on it, turned it to the right, and tried to push the door open. It didn't budge. She tried turning it to the left, heard a click, and the door handle turned in her small hand.

"Hey, what are you doing there?"

Sophie jumped when she heard the voice calling from the other end of the hallway. She failed to notice the two men until they were walking down the hall toward her. One of the men snickered at the curious and scared little girl.

"Hey, do you know the secret code word to get in there?" he asked in a playful tone.

Sophie shook her head.

"Then I guess you better get back upstairs," he said gently.

Sophie ran back upstairs.

That must have been the Indigo Room. I wasn't allowed in back then.

Sophie moved on to the kitchen with her checklist. Justin came in through the door in the back of the kitchen that went out to the alley behind the building where the dumpster was. He had just returned from taking some items out to the trash.

"There you are. Thought you disappeared again," Sophie said.

"What do you mean?" Justin asked.

Sophie thought now would be as good a time as any to confront him. "Charlie mentioned that you keep disappearing on her. You left the hotel the other night and she woke up and you weren't there. Then you were gone so long last night."

"I had something to take care of," Justin said vaguely.

"In the middle of the night?" Sophie was getting annoyed

remembering how the girl was alone when she first discovered her.

"Yes, and I wasn't far," Justin said.

"I know it's not my concern, but she should be your concern. I mean, do you need help with something? Someone to watch her or money? Whatever I can help with," Sophie said.

"Yes, she is my concern, and yes I could use some help," Justin said calmly.

He peeked in on Charlie who was sitting on the stool coloring and watching a movie on Sophie's tablet, wearing headphones that were almost bigger than her head.

"Okay?" Sophie said, waiting for his request.

"I need your car," Justin said.

"My car?"

"You remember I mentioned my friend owns the auto shop around the corner."

"Yes," Sophie said.

"Well, I have been working on something over there off and on for a few days."

"What have you been working on?"

"Charlie's birthday is coming up. Well, it's still a few months away, but I built her a toy box. I was trying to finish it in time or at least when I had time and a place to work on it. I wasn't sure what our next few months would look like. I need your car to pick it up."

"Of course. Yes." Sophie was surprised at his answer, feeling a little guilty for assuming several other reasons for his absence.

"She was fine here. I wasn't far and I just wanted to make her something special. She's never had one and she hasn't had many toys lately. I wanted her to have something for her bedroom. Once I found a bedroom for her. To make it appear more permanent. You know? Something that is hers. But I also didn't want to raise any questions with anyone, so she was safest here and then with you at the hotel," Justin said.

Sophie smiled and nodded in understanding, realizing that given the circumstances, maybe he made the best decision he could.

"I'm sure she will love it," Sophie said.

Charlie interrupted them with technical difficulties. Something popped up on the tablet that disrupted her movie. Sophie reached for the tablet and noticed an article. She zeroed in on the words Blue Owl. It had information about the legend of the hauntings. She didn't remember coming across that particular article in earlier research.

Sensing from the furrowed brow on Sophie's face that it was more serious than just pressing a button to restart the movie, Justin asked, "What is it?"

Sophie was quickly scanning the article but didn't want to read it in front of Charlie.

"Charlie, why don't you see if you can find something else to play with for a few minutes until we get this figured out," Justin said.

"Okay." The little girl skipped off back to her coloring book and crayons for a few minutes and then decided to look in the room where the few things she had were kept.

"Strange, I don't remember having this tab open. It's an article. According to this, the hauntings of the Blue Owl may be linked to a little girl named Hazel. She died in this building back in the late 1920s. It shows a picture of her," Sophie said, holding the tablet up to Justin to see the picture.

"What happened to her?"

"It says she was found locked in the storage room of the cellar. Some kind of trauma to the head was the cause of death," Sophie said.

"That's awful! So, is she the ghost that Jamison and Mae were talking about?" Justin asked, sounding skeptical of the supernatural events.

"I guess so." Sophie said, zooming in on the picture.

Charlie came back into the room carrying an old stuffed animal. A tan colored lion with worn matted material and a dark brown mane, equally matted. The green, marbled eyes were still intact.

"Found something," Charlie said as she proudly held up the stuffed lion.

Sophie and Justin looked at the lion. Recognition set in as they glanced in disbelief at each other and then back at the picture on the tablet of the little girl, Hazel, holding a stuffed lion with the same matted and worn look. Chills set in as they were hesitant to ask Charlie where she found the lion, suspecting an answer they were not ready for.

"Nice lion," Justin said. "Where'd ya find that little guy?" he tried to ask casually.

"My friend said I could play with it."

"Friend?" Justin asked. "And what does this friend look like?"

"Umm, she doesn't have the same hair as me. It's shorter than mine and it's the same as my brown crayon. She said I could have him," Charlie said.

"Do you know your friend's name?" Sophie asked.

"I can't remember, but she said she used to live here like I do," Charlie said.

"Does she look like this little girl in the picture?" Sophie asked, turning the tablet around so Charlie could see the picture.

"Yeah, that's her!"

"And you saw her? Here?" Justin asked.

"Yeah, just now, in the other room and another time when Daddy was gone." Charlie said innocently.

Sophie and Justin exchanged a look, unsure whether or not to pursue more questions that were on their minds. Justin shook his head as if to signal her to hold off.

"Well, that was nice of her to give the little lion to you," Sophie said.

"Let me know if you see your friend again, alright?" Justin said with concern.

"I will," Charlie said.

All these unexplained events had Sophie's interest piqued. The car window, the flickering lights in the ladies' room, Charlie's new friend and the lion, the haunting dream that she had been having, and the woman in the photograph. The newly acquired building certainly came with its share of mysteries. Sophie was sure there had to be an explanation, a connection. Her curiosity led her to delve into the past in search of information that would explain some of these mysteries. She pulled out her laptop, hopped up on a stool, and was thankful for all the information available at her fingertips. Justin was working on fixing the old jukebox while Sophie was busy surfing the net for information. She was searching for anything that might help link these mysteries together. Her verbal reaction to another article caught Justin's attention. He came over to see what she had found and leaned in to see the screen, his hand on the back of her chair. She was too intrigued at the moment to give attention to the building energy between them.

"Listen to this," Sophie said softly in case of small listening ears. "In 1929, a girl named Hazel Mackenzie went missing and was later found dead, locked in a cellar storage room. Hazel was the daughter of one of the owners of the Blue Owl. There were several rumors about what happened to her, but nobody knows for sure. There were suspicions surrounding her death," Sophie said.

"What suspicions?" Justin asked.

"At first, the parents were suspected because they didn't call authorities right away when she went missing. If they did, maybe she would have been found alive," Sophie said.

"If the Blue Owl was moonlighting as a speakeasy back then, maybe they didn't want to risk being found out. Calling the police to come search the building may not have sounded like a good first choice," Justin said.

"Especially if they thought she just wandered off," Sophie added.

"Unless they did have something to do with it," Justin added.

"Oh wait, it says they ruled the parents out and that it may have been an accident. Everything in the storage room was destroyed, bottles smashed. They think she was trying to make some noise to get help or went crazy being locked in," Sophie said.

"Can't blame her for that," Justin said.

"What a place to be. She was only seven years old." Sophie looked up in horror, realizing that Charlie and Sam were about that age too.

"How well do you know Jamison?" Justin asked.

"About as well as you do, I guess. I just met him when I inherited the place. He was walking Chili and stopped in when he saw the open door," Sophie said.

"He knows a lot about this place and its history. I'm just surprised he didn't mention that information at dinner. I don't know about you, but I got an impression that he was holding back," Justin said.

"No, I didn't really notice. I was distracted. Between the headache and then seeing the photo of the lady with the dark hair," Sophie said.

"Lady with the dark hair? Do you know her?" Justin asked.

"Okay, this is going to sound crazy." Sophie said.

"Hey, no judgement from me. It will fit right in with everything else going on around here," Justin said.

"Well, I have been having these dreams for the past few months. The same lady in them. Asking me the same question.

Did you find the key? It's disturbing. Anyway, the lady in the photo is the same as the one in my dream. Creepy huh?" Sophie asked.

"Whoo," he said, shaking his head. "You have some vivid dreams."

"Tell me about it. I think I'd rather just not remember them," Sophie said.

"Well, there must be a reason for it. Do you have someone in your head shrinking world that analyzes dreams or some hocus pocus that can help?" Justin asked.

"No," Sophie said, letting out a slight laugh of amusement. "We don't really practice hocus pocus anymore. It's outdated. But I might have someone I can call that may be able to help." She grabbed her cell phone and called Harlan Reed. He was an expert on the city's history of that era, especially after all the research for Grayce's party. Maybe he knew something that would help.

Harlan was eager to help her. He told Sophie he would do some digging and make a few calls to some of his friends. They scheduled a lunch date for the next day at the diner down the street from Sophie's building. He insisted on coming to her and was confident that he could find something out by then. It was the least he could do for all her work with Grayce's birthday party. Plus, he wanted to see the location of her new venture.

By the time Sophie finished her phone call with Harlan, Justin almost had the jukebox fixed. He was re-assembling the last of the pieces and wiping it down with a rag.

"So, who's Harlan?" Justin asked after overhearing the phone conversation.

"A very handsome, rich, and highly intelligent man I am considering running off with," Sophie said dramatically in a playful tone.

"Oh?" A hint of uncertainty in his voice. Not knowing Harlan, Justin assumed she was joking, but not certain.

"You're welcome to join us tomorrow if you want," Sophie said.

"What about Charlie? I don't think I should," Justin said.

"I have a perfect solution! My friend Marcella has a little boy Charlie's age. I was going to call her anyway. She happens to be out of work at the moment. I'll see if she's available tomorrow. Charlie and Sam can have a play date or whatever they are calling it these days. If that's good with you." Before Justin could answer, Sophie switched gears in her mind. "Wait! She is out of work at the moment."

"Okay?" Justin inquired.

"We are looking for a bartender. It just occurred to me. She would be perfect for the job!" Sophie said.

"Alright, sounds like you have it all figured out. You seem like a woman on a mission. Don't want to get in the way of that." Holding his hands up in surrender. "Plus, I'd like to meet this man you're running off with." He smiled at Sophie, giving her a slight wink.

"Wine?" Sophie asked.

"I'm more of a beer and whiskey guy, but sure," Justin said.

"I'll have to remember that for next time." Sophie said.

Sophie commented on how nice the jukebox looked now that it was cleaned up and put back together, without its insides sprawled out on the floor. She brought over a glass of wine for him and took a sip of her own. Justin mentioned that it had a few minor electrical issues and with a few tweaks it was good as new. While Justin was pushing last minute buttons on the jukebox to test it out, Sophie noticed that Charlie had fallen asleep on the couch across the room. She went over to take the tablet out of her tiny hand and gently move her arm to a more comfortable position without disturbing her. The blanket was over by the bar stool. Justin saw what Sophie was doing and smiled with appreciation for the care and concern she had shown his daughter. He was closer in proximity to the blanket. He walked over and lifted it off the stool without breaking his stride and took it over to her.

As he moved toward them, the jukebox reset and a song started to play. Sophie recognized it from the first two notes and the gentle twang of the guitar. It was one of those songs that has a distinct beginning. "Wicked Game" by Chris Isaac was one of her favorites. The provocative rhythm was pleasing to her ears. Justin laid the blanket down over Charlie. Sophie leaned in and straightened the end of the blanket closest to her. Their hands met and overlapped, touching softly. Inches from each other, they could both feel the pull. A spark of interest igniting between them. Justin breathed in the scent of her light, floral perfume. She could see the slight, rough stubble on his face and neck, which she envisioned running her hand over but didn't dare reach up toward him as her body was urging her to do. They glanced at each other briefly before Sophie started to pull her hand back. Justin smiled warmly and reached for her hand before she pulled it completely away. He nodded his head in the direction of what would be the dance floor area. Sophie raised her eyebrows in a questioning manner.

"Gotta try it out. Make sure it's, you know, safe," Justin said.

"Well, for quality control purposes then." She smiled back, fighting the contradiction of desire and hesitance, along with the anticipation of knowing in a few seconds she would be in very close proximity to him. *Maybe this isn't safe.*

He pulled her in toward him. Sophie put her hand on his upper arm, sliding her hand upward to find a secure position. Touching the firm curves of his shoulder in the process was a bad idea. It was strong under the palm of her hand. His crisp white t-shirt was the only barrier between his skin and her fingertips. A hint of sandalwood fragranced soap was still mixed with his scent making it even more difficult and pleasant to be so close to him. She wasn't sure if it was the wine, the music, or the company that captivated her. She could be mesmerized in the moment forever, but she knew better. *He is not part of the plan. How can I feel this way about someone I just met and know so little about?*

Trying to avoid the obvious chemistry between them in that moment, Justin broke the ice. "Thanks for all your help with Charlie. She really likes you."

"Oh, of course," Sophie said, snapping out of momentary bliss. "And thank you for all your help with the cleaning and fixing stuff. You're pretty talented with a hammer."

"You should see me with a chinois?"

Sophie gave a quizzical look. "Huh?"

"For cooking." Justin said.

"Yeah, Yeah, I knew that. Just not what I thought you'd say," Sophie said.

"Uh huh," Justin said skeptically. "What were you hoping for?" Justin said as he pulled her in a little closer.

Then before she answered, he pushed her away, still holding one hand. With a dancing motion, he slowly twirled her around, reeled her back in, and dipped her over his arm. Pulling her back up, his hand rested gently on her lower back. Their bodies swayed rhythmically with the music. Every muscle in his firm body was tense as he guided her around the small dance floor with unwavering confidence until she looked into his eyes. In that moment he became a desirable combination of strength and vulnerability at the same time.

They locked eyes, enchanted by the seductive music and the moment between them. Justin leaned in slowly, closer and closer to her face. Sophie moved her head toward his as if her mind was no longer in control and her body had taken over. Their lips met softly. He gently kissed her as she returned the movement and pressed her lips into his. They recovered from the moment and realized where they were. A smile sparked with unfinished business in their eyes. Noticing movement, Justin glanced across the room. Charlie woke up and was walking over to join them.

CHAPTER 23

Marcella swooped by the Blue Owl in the morning with Sam and Max, who insisted on joining them to pick up Charlotte. She wasn't sure who was more excited for a fun-filled, kid-friendly day, her son or her older brother who in some ways never grew up. Knowing her brother all too well, she suspected an additional motive to his desire to nurture his adolescent self. She suspected Max wanted to meet Sophie's new head of security and handyman who was labeled by Sophie as annoying squatter just a few days ago.

Marcella had a way of entering a room full force. She was difficult to ignore since she had an innate way of taking charge. She skipped over superficial pleasantries, right to the substance. As if being a working single mom left her no time to waste on idle chit chat.

"Wow, Soph. This is charming," Marcella said with genuine excitement. "I know you said it needed some work, but I can see the potential here. So, you're keeping it?"

"I'm going to give it a try. Not sure it's the right time but we will see," Sophie said.

"Ahh, there's never a right time. Sometimes you just have to go for it," Max said.

Sophie introduced Marcella, Sam, and Max to Justin and Charlotte. Sam and Charlie hit it off right away as if they had always known each other. They had already broken off from the group and Sam was showing her a game on his tablet.

"So how do I get the grand tour?" Max asked, breaking the ice.

Marcella gave Sophie an approving look that she had eyed Justin up and down and noticed his good looks. Max smirked and laughed to himself, recognizing the girls involved with a language of their own.

"Justin, why don't you show me around. You've been living here recently, right?" Max said with a hint of polite sarcasm.

"Uh, yes, shall we start with the east wing?" Justin said, giving it right back to Max.

They all took the quick tour around the building and up to the apartment units. Marcella hung back slightly, to quietly inquire about the new possibility for Sophie. Marcella was hinting at more than just the business opportunity.

"I barely know him. Plus, he has a complicated situation with his daughter and his interest should be there," Sophie said.

"So, there's interest on your part?" Marcella asked.

"I do have interest in something. I am looking for a bartender. Since you're out of a job, I thought you might consider the offer?" Sophie asked.

"Well, I'll need to know what the compensation and benefits package is," Marcella said playfully.

"I'll have someone from HR contact you," Sophie said.

As they all caught up together after the short tour, Max made a comment about Marcella working for Sophie, since she needed a job.

"Max, you're two minutes behind," Marcella said.

"Alright, who's ready for some FUN today?" Max asked the kids with excitement.

"Meeee!" Sam bellowed.

"I am!" Charlie exclaimed at the same time.

"Let's get this party started! We will see YOU two later," Marcella said, looking at Justin and then Sophie, giving her a wink. "You kids have fun. I'll call you later, Soph."

"Okay, bye," Sophie said.

"Nice to meet you," Justin said as they were heading out the door.

Justin turned to Sophie, asking, "So, what was the wink for?" pretending he had no idea.

"Yeah, I don't know what that was," Sophie said, avoiding the conversation. She turned her arm up as if to look at a watch on her wrist that didn't exist. "Oh, look at the time. We should get to the diner."

Justin and Sophie walked down to the diner on the corner to meet Harlan Reed for lunch. Sophie was curious to find out what information Harlan was able to find. All three of them arrived together on the corner, just outside the door. After introductions and a brief recap by Harlan about the work Sophie had done for his wife's party, they entered and headed for an open booth. The enticing smell of the day's grilled specials passed by on a serving tray.

Sophie gave Harlan an update on all the recent changes in her life since they had seen each other a week ago. The job falling through, the relationship with Logan falling through, her new inheritance from a patient, the photo she got from Jamison of the lady from the dream she was having, and the haunted tales of the Blue Owl. Sophie also mentioned the information she found on Hazel at the time she called him.

"I did some digging of my own," Harlan said. "You already know the building that you inherited was called the Blue Owl. There were three original owners back in the late 1920s and early 30s. Eddie Stone, Macie Brooks, and Roselyn Mackenzie were friends and business partners. After a few years, Eddie was forced to take over the major responsibilities. Macie suddenly left town and Roselyn was distraught after the loss of her child, Hazel. The Stone family kept the business running until the late 90s with various family members managing it but keeping the Blue Owl name. Then it sat vacant for several years. Ownership was passed to Ezra Stone, Eddie's son, after Eddie passed away."

"Seems strange Macie would take off, leave town, and leave her friends to deal with the grief and the business on their own," Sophie said.

"Rumors are that either there was some falling out between them, or the loss was too great for her as well, being so close," Harlan added.

"Maybe she had to leave for another business opportunity? If the business was failing or if there was a falling out between the partners," Justin said.

"Unless she knew something about Hazel's death and wanted get as far away as she could," Sophie said.

"Roselyn Mackenzie had another child besides Hazel. That child grew up and had a family of her own. One of her children later became Vivian Thomas after getting married," Harlan said.

"My mother," Sophie said.

"Sophie, Roselyn Mackenzie was your great-grandmother," Harlan said.

"I don't even know what to say," Sophie said.

"That means, our ghost Hazel would be your great-aunt," Justin said.

"Well, it gets better. I have a photograph of Roselyn Mackenzie." Harlan slid the photo across the table toward Sophie.

She immediately recognized the woman in the photo. It was the same photo she saw at Jamison's house. The same face that had been haunting her dreams and appeared in the reflection of the car window. The woman who kept asking the question, "did you find the key?" She told them about the dream and the haunting words.

"Is it a message from beyond?" Sophie realized how silly she sounded after saying it out loud. "And what key?"

"Maybe it's a literal key, like the one missing that opens the cellar door?" said Justin.

"Or it could be a figurative key. Some clue leading to more information. Some unsolved mystery," Harlan said.

"What is there still to solve?" asked Sophie.

"You said there was some suspicion surrounding Hazel's death, right? Well, what if it wasn't an accident? What if the parents did have something to do with it?" Justin said.

"But if they did, what would your great-grandmother be leading you to find out? Wouldn't she want to keep you from the truth?" Harlan said.

"True. But what if she didn't have anything to do with it? What if it was another family member? Maybe someone else, one of the patrons, was unstable or irate?" Sophie said.

"There must be something you still need to discover," Harlan said.

"If there is a clue or something, how do you even know it's in the building? After all this time, would there even be anything to find?" Justin asked.

"We need to get into that cellar and take a look around. Maybe something down there will help us find out," Sophie said. "That is the only place I haven't been able to access yet."

When the food arrived at the table, they paused the conversation for a few minutes. Sophie put her napkin in her lap and took a few bites of her club sandwich. Justin was busy putting ketchup on his burger and fries. After setting up his Greek salad with dressing, and cutting it into more manageable bites, Harlan politely flagged down the server for beverage refills for all three of them.

"Maybe Jamison knows something more. Justin, you said you thought he held something back at dinner the other night," Sophie said.

"Yeah. I can't say for sure, but it was just a gut feeling I got. Can you trust him?" Justin asked.

"Why would he hide anything from us?" Sophie asked.

Their attention shifted to the person standing at the edge of their table. They expected the server coming back for refills; instead, it was Jamison standing there. He happened to be in the neighborhood. They wondered how much of their conversation he heard as he approached the table. Leaving Sophie on edge, there was a quick awkward pause before she interrupted with introductions. Jamison's tone and actions implied his normal behavior, so perhaps Sophie was concerned for nothing.

Sophie debated for a second whether to confront him now or let it go. If he did hear them, and he did have something to hide, why not lay all the cards on the table and get to the bottom of it. Just as she was going to lead with a question, Justin put his hand on her knee under the table to stop her. She was taken by surprise but understood his intention. He must have had intuition not to divulge information they just learned. They waited until Jamison was out the door with his carry out order before they continued their conversation.

"Jamison's last name is Brooks, isn't it?" Justin asked.

"Yes," Sophie said, realizing where he was going with the question. "Yes, it is. What if he is involved somehow? Maybe you were right to think he knew more than he mentioned."

If Jamison did have more information, she had to find out what he was holding on to. She didn't even know if there was something to find after all this time, but it became an even more personal quest now that her family was involved. The history, the secrets, the mystery behind it all. Sophie intended to find out.

CHAPTER 24

Later that afternoon, she hurried back to check the cellar door again. Still locked. *Seriously? What was I expecting? Ghosts to unlock it?* She went through all the keys that were given to her at the attorney's office. None of them unlocked the door. Sophie and Justin searched around, in drawers, on shelves, hoping there would be an extra key lying around. Nothing.

"You could call a locksmith to open it and change the lock so you would have a key," Justin suggested.

"They didn't teach you lock picking skills in the military?" Sophie said.

"Why pick the lock when you have fire power. Much faster," Justin said.

"Good point," Sophie said. "Maybe I'll wait for the locksmith."

Sophie found a number online and set up an appointment for a local locksmith to come out the next day. She was bursting with anticipation to see what was down there but had to put her curiosity on hold. There was still unpacking to do.

The one thing she did not have to wait on any longer was moving into an apartment. Finally, a new home to look forward to, even if it was potentially haunted. The rest of the day was spent settling into the apartments. Arranging and rearranging furniture for best function. Decorating her bathroom with new accessories, including a new black and white celestial-themed shower curtain, black rugs creating contrast to the white subway tile in the shower and the white and black floor tile. She brought some color into the room with a bright yellow towel on the towel rack and a small vase on the counter with coordinating yellow artificial flowers.

The last of her things were finally unpacked in her bedroom. Sophie looked around the room with satisfaction. Her new bed, covered in a fluffy down comforter with a white and gray pinstriped duvet cover, coordinated with the freshly painted pewter gray walls with white trim. The only thing missing was some artwork for the walls. One of the old dressers she had found and cleaned up had a vintage charm to it. She decided to refinish it to bring in a bold color to the room, making it an accent piece.

Her thoughts drifted to the toy box that Justin made for Charlie. She decided to go check on their move in progress. Even though they didn't have much to move in, Sophie made sure they had all the basics. She set her empty boxes on the landing at the top of the stairs and entered the apartment across the hall. Sophie joined them in Charlie's new room while they were in the middle of putting her new sheets on the bed. Justin was lofting the top sheet in the air to cover the bed and Charlie hopped under it. He saw Sophie come in and smiled.

"I think there's something wrong with this bed. I keep trying to make it but there's a lump in it," Justin said as he sat lightly on the giggling lump.

Charlie peeked her head out of the sheet. "Sophie! Do you like my new bedroom?"

"It's beautiful! I love it!" Sophie said.

"Eh, it's well enough," Justin said with deflating enthusiasm. "It is missing one thing, though."

"What?" Charlie asked.

"Hmm, I'll be right back." Justin said.

Justin hurried down the stairs between the apartments, through the storefront area, and headed to the storage room off the kitchen. As he entered the room, he heard movement by the front door. Moving closer to investigate, he was in time to see the front door move slightly and then close. Quickly pulling the door open, he looked around for possible intruders that he may have just missed. Nobody was around except a few sidewalk stragglers down the block. Too far away to have just left the building. Justin closed and locked the door. He thought maybe it was the wind moving a slightly open door which was a more comforting thought than any paranormal activity. Back on track after a slight distraction, Justin continued to find the carefully hidden toy box he made for Charlie. He uncovered the handcrafted wooden box, swiftly picked it up, and effortlessly carried it back up to the apartment. When he entered the bedroom and set it on the floor against the wall, Charlie ran over to it.

"Is that for me?" Charlie asked, her eyes wide, smiling from ear to ear.

"I know your birthday is a few months away still, but I thought this would be a good time to give it to you," Justin said.

"You made this?" Sophie asked, admiring the beautiful craftsmanship and the style. It was an antique white toy box with a slightly distressed element. The name Charlotte was neatly hand painted in large, charcoal gray curved print on the front.

Charlie hopped off the bed and quickly made her way to the box, not hesitating to open the lid. "It's so big, I can fit in it!"

"You can fit all your toys in it," Justin said.

Charlie suddenly frowned with concern. "Oh, I only have a couple of toys."

"How about if we change that? We can go to the store on your birthday and pick some new ones out," Sophie said. "If it's okay with your dad."

"Really? Can we Daddy?" Charlie's excitement returned.

"Yes, we can, Jellybean, but first we need to get you settled and ready for bed. But you can dream about all the new toys to pick from," Justin said.

Sophie said good night to them and realized how exhausted she was. She went back across the hall to her apartment and opened a bottle of wine in celebration of her new home. She poured herself a glass of Riesling, sat on her new couch, and enjoyed both for a while.

Her new surroundings were a little strange, more unfamiliar. It would take a bit to adjust. The thought of going to sleep at the moment was put off with thinking about ghosts and secrets and hidden clues. She poured another glass of wine hoping to push it all away for the evening but the anticipation of searching the cellar crept back in. The curiosity won out. She wandered downstairs and found herself standing in front of the cellar door. Against her better judgement, knowing the door was still locked and the locksmith would be there the next day, she ventured over to the cellar door anyway. She closed her eyes before reaching for the door handle. Almost as if she was trying to will the door to open. Sophie carefully gripped the handle. Slowly turning the knob, expecting it to stop as it did the past few times, she tried to open it. This time she was surprised that the handle kept turning and just after a click, the door opened. *Can ghosts open doors? Must be too much wine, or not enough.* She opened it a crack and complete darkness crept out of the other side of the door. Nighttime. By herself. Armed with her cell phone flashlight and a half glass of wine. In her pajamas. Unexplained legends of a ghost. *Definitely not enough wine to go down there, at the moment.*

A muffled, repetitious pounding came from behind her. It

was across the room, near the kitchen. She followed the sound and saw a light on in the kitchen storage room. Justin was punching a heavy bag that hung in the corner. Each blow muffled by a pair of gray boxing gloves. *That explains the good shape he is in.* She didn't want to interrupt his training, plus she was enjoying the view. No sneak peeks. This time, the shirt was completely off.

Leaning against the doorway with a relaxed confidence, Sophie believed she had the element of surprise this time. He would be the one flustered. Justin saw movement out of the corner of his eye when she took a sip from her wine glass. There was something alluring to him about the way Sophie was casually leaning against the wall in her pajama pants and tank top. Justin stopped hitting the bag and acknowledged her with a smile. Catching his breath, he took off his boxing gloves, dropped them to the floor, and slowly walked over to Sophie, not breaking eye contact. He was standing inches from her. She was waiting with intense focus to see what his next move was going to be. He reached for her wine glass and slipped it out of her hand. Then downed the rest of the contents in the glass. He slid his other hand around her waist to the small of her back. In one swift motion, he pulled her in toward him and firmly kissed her. Sliding the tip of his tongue just inside her lips. Locked together in motion for seconds, not long enough for either of them, he pulled back slightly.

"I didn't want you to spill your wine," Justin said.

"So thoughtful of you," Sophie said.

"Speaking of thoughtful, I have something for you," Justin said.

"You're going to refill my glass?" Sophie said.

"Much better than that," Justin said.

He walked back over to the heavy bag and against the wall behind it was a box with a red ribbon on it. Sophie followed him over and took the box that he held out for her. She pulled one end of the red ribbon and the knot slipped out. She pulled the lid off the box, exposing a pair of red boxing gloves. She took them out, setting the box on the floor, and admired them more closely. The smooth, bold red of the glove contrasted with the wide, white Velcro tab with black writing.

"I thought we could work on a few moves." Pointing to the bag, "Protection and stress relief," Justin said.

"You sound like you have experience with this," Sophie said.

"Let's just say I found myself in a few situations that were over my head when I was younger. A little too confident ended up being a lack of ability, which I found out soon enough. I did get to keep this scar on my shoulder as a consolation prize. Then, I was lucky enough to cross paths with someone that took an interest or took pity on me and decided to help train me. My initial resistance made it no easy task. But eventually, he got through," Justin said.

"Well, it's good he was able to put all that energy to a purpose," Sophie said. "Did that have something to do with your interest in the Marines?" Sophie asked as she slipped her hands into the boxing gloves and fastened the tabs.

"I'm sure it had something to do with it," Justin said.

"Thank you for the gloves." She held up her hands, showing off her new accessories. "So, let's see some moves. Show me whatcha got!" Sophie said.

"Ladies first," Justin said as he guided Sophie to the heavy bag. "Do you trust me?" Justin asked.

"The last time I trusted someone, they made arrangements for a different life and forgot to tell me," Sophie said indignantly.

"Well, you've already mastered lesson one," Justin said.

"I have? What was lesson one again?" Sophie asked.

"Fuel," Justin said.

"Ah, I see. Channel frustration into something productive," Sophie said.

"That's what's great about that bag. It always takes what you have to give," Justin said.

"And for lesson two?" Sophie asked.

"Never underestimate your opponent," Justin said as he stepped behind her leg with his left foot while pushing her shoulder backward. Literally sweeping her off her feet but catching her just before she landed on the ground.

As he helped her regain her balance, she planted her left foot carefully behind his right foot then reached out for him. Suddenly shifting her weight, lowering her center of gravity, and pushing into him. He lost his balance and stumbled backward onto the ground.

"I'm a quick study," Sophie said as Justin looked at her both surprised and pleased.

"I see you've mastered lesson two as well," he said.

She reached out to help him up. The lights went out. It was completely dark. Sophie took the boxing gloves off and found her cell phone flashlight.

"I'll check the breaker box," Justin said. "Actually, it's probably on the lower level which we can't get to until tomorrow."

"No, I was meaning to ask you. When I first came down here, I checked the door again just to see. It was unlocked. Did you find the key?" Sophie asked, realizing the irony as soon as the words left her mouth.

"Hmmm. No, I didn't find a key, but that's strange," Justin said.

"What's strange?" Sophie asked.

"When I came down here earlier to get the toy box for Charlie, I thought I saw movement by the front door. Like someone had just closed it when I came in," Justin said.

"Do you think there was someone in here?" Sophie asked.

"I didn't see anyone around," Justin said.

With the flashlight leading their way, they went to check

the cellar door. It was unlocked, just as Sophie said.

"But how would it have gotten unlocked?" Sophie asked.

"Apparently strange things happen around here," Justin said.

"So, I've heard," Sophie said.

"Who would have a key and what would they want?" Justin asked.

"Yeah." Sophie agreed with his line of questioning. "More mysteries to solve."

CHAPTER 25

"There it is," Justin said. He swiped the cobwebs out of the way and opened the panel door to the breaker box that was in the cellar. Sophie shined her light from the old-world, heavy wood door with black metal trim around to the breaker box, exposing more details of the room. The small storage area was lined with metal shelving which contained boxes, some empty liquor bottles, old rags, and other miscellaneous items scattered around. A few clicks later, "We have light!"

"Great! Now we can get out of here. I get a weird vibe in this room. Very gloomy. Like the walls are closing in on you," Sophie said.

"Lead the way," Justin said.

Sophie couldn't move. She was staring at the doorway of the small storage room they were in. Justin looked at Sophie. "What is it? Do I even wanna know?"

"You don't see that?" She could barely get the whisper out.

Justin cautiously shifted his eyes toward the image blocking their exit. A strange, almost translucent image of a little girl that dissipated into the dim light from the hallway.

"Hazel?" Sophie called out. Nothing but silence returned. She turned to Justin. "That had to be her. Same dark hair and green eyes from the picture in the article."

"I'm not sure what I just saw but there is definitely some

kind of energy down here," Justin said.

"I'm not sure if that was the most fascinating thing or the scariest thing I've seen. Either way I'm ready to get out of this cellar," Sophie said.

"Agreed. The sooner, the better," Justin said.

"We can take the shortcut," Sophie said, leading Justin back up to the kitchen and up through the trap door to her apartment.

"This comes in handy," Justin said, climbing up the ladder.

Sophie walked him to the door of her apartment. Neither of them wanted to call it a night between the paranormal energy and the energy building between them. A few seconds of silence left uncertainty if the other was interested.

"I have a couple of beers in my fridge if you want one," Justin said.

"That actually sounds good. I'll take you up on it," Sophie said.

Sitting at the kitchen table in Justin's apartment, Sophie picked up the ice cold can and cracked the tab open. Raising the can to her lips, the cool amber liquid hit her tongue, filling her mouth.

"That's the best part, isn't it?" Justin asked.

"The first sip? Especially if it's cold," Sophie said.

Justin cracked open his beer and held it up. "To the unexpected."

"To unexpected opportunities," Sophie said, clinking her can to his then taking a sip. Their eye contact lingered for a few extra seconds. Sophie interrupted with a subject change.

"That night at Jamison's house, when we all had dinner together. Do you remember that strange phone call?" Sophie asked.

Justin shook his head. "No. What call was that?"

"Mae and I were in the kitchen. Jamison's cell phone rang and Mae answered it. Her tone and her body language changed.

She sounded bothered by the caller," Sophie said.

"I still think he withheld something that night," Justin said.

"It's strange," Sophie said, pondering what he could have kept from them.

"What's strange?" Justin asked.

"Well, with him having all those photos and mentioning how much information he had—they both had—about the history, why wouldn't he mention if he was related to one of the original owners," Sophie said.

"And if that's true, how would he not know the name of the lady in the photograph he gave you. Of your great grandmother," Justin said.

"Or even that Hazel, the spirit of the little girl, clearly haunting the building, was her daughter," Sophie added.

"Do you think he had another agenda for offering the partnership?" Justin asked.

"Like, to gain access to the building without causing suspicion?" Sophie asked. "It's all speculation. Maybe it was a coincidence that he walked his dog by this building every day. Maybe he was just interested in another renovation project," Sophie said, not convinced that it was coincidental.

"My intuition disagrees with you," Justin said.

"Yeah, I'm with you. I'm trying to give him the benefit of the doubt, but I just don't know him that well." Sophie said.

"If there is something he wants, we don't know how far he is willing to go to get it. He may be dangerous," Justin warned her.

"That's why, if there is something to be found, we need to find it first," Sophie said.

CHAPTER 26

Daylight couldn't come fast enough for Sophie. She fought the urge to run down to the cellar in her pajamas, sporting bed head and morning breath to start the search, even after the Hazel sighting last night, wondering if there was anything to find after all these years. After a quick shower and the fifteen-minute version of hair and make-up, Sophie opted for the quickest route to the cellar door. She opened the trap door in the back of her apartment to the secret passage that led to the Blue Owl bar. She carefully climbed through the opening in the floor and down the ladder, landing her not so stark white Converse shoes in the kitchen storage room. As she quickly pivoted away from the ladder, the pant leg of her jeans caught on an old, rusty nail sticking out of the side of the ladder. The momentum caused a slight rip in the cuff of her light blue jeans. Reaching for anything to catch her balance, she stumbled onto a nearby shelf, knocking a leftover can of mahogany wood stain onto the floor. The stain splattered onto her white V-neck T-shirt. After the initial shock, she looked around for a rag or towel, anything to wipe off the stain. There was a rag on the lower shelf. Grabbing it out of the box and wiping her shirt just spread the stain around. She was able to absorb some of the liquid to reduce the dampness. She ignored the cold sticky feel of the clinging t-shirt. She quickly wiped up the small amount on the floor, the majority landing on her shirt. Sophie continued on her mission. Passing through the doorway, her mind and body fluttered with lascivious thoughts of the previous night's intense interaction with Justin.

Outside the door to the cellar, she paused for a moment, unsure she wanted to venture down there. Her hands starting to sweat and her pulse quickening. Armed with a flashlight and a sober mind, Sophie decided that finding out the truth that may provide answers was pushing her forward. As she reached down to the door handle, she noticed the door was the slightest bit cracked open. She pulled the door the rest of the way open and reached in to flick on the light at the top of the stairway. Cautiously but steadily descending the stairs one at a time, she pressed the power button on her flashlight. The added lighting exposed the cobwebs above her head. At the bottom of the stairway, she found another light switch to illuminate the hallway. To the left, there was a closed door opposite the stairway, a few feet of hallway between them. There was a longer hallway to the right with a door on the opposite side, near the end. That door was open, and a light was shining into the hallway. The light leading her in that direction, she started down the hall toward the room. She figured Justin had gotten an early start and made his way down there since their search was cut short last night. The musty scent in the air combined with the fumes from the spattered stain hit and suddenly tickled her nose. She tried to hold back a sneeze. The burning on the inside of her nose built until the velocity of the blow could not be contained.

Walking down the hallway, ghostly thoughts churned in her mind. The dark, crypt-like underground area had its own level of creepiness. Not to mention the paranormal activity that she had recently heard stories about, as well as witnessed herself. She was imagining all the people that had walked through the same hall over the years. Thinking back to the pictures that Jamison had from back in the 1920s during pro-hibition. Having to hide underground or in a back room some-where to be served alcohol. Secret passwords and threats of getting caught and arrested. This was the room they talked about. This was the Indigo Room. The room she saw a hint of as a child. One that she now owned and was part of her fam-ily's history. Slight uneasiness mixed with excitement set in as she came within proximity of the door.

The door was three-quarters of the way open, enough room for her to enter without having to push it open. Sophie was surprised at how small the room actually was compared to how she imagined it would be. It had an underground charm with its exposed brick walls and the sleek, simple, wood bar top against the back wall. The bar itself was not near as elaborate as the one on the level above but it was functional for its purpose. She continued scanning the room from just inside the door. The furniture, consisting of a few high-back accent chairs and short round tables to her left, was pushed together with some randomly placed stragglers. To her right there was movement from behind the door. Sophie reached for the edge of the door and moved it toward her, exposing whatever was lurking behind the door.

"Jamison! What are you doing here?" Sophie was startled by the unexpected visitor. The fact that he was hiding behind the door made Sophie question his intentions and mental state. She tried to casually take a few steps away from him, trying to create more distance without showing signs of her uneasiness.

Jamison looked either just as startled to see her or guilty that he was caught. "Just getting an idea of the renovations," he said nervously. He took a few steps toward her.

"Really? Hiding behind the door? How did you even get in here?"

"The key you gave me," Jamison said.

"I didn't have a key," Sophie said with suspicion that he may have had the key the whole time.

"I think it's time for you to leave," Sophie said firmly, despite the anxiousness in the pit of her stomach and the quickening of her pulse.

"I can't," Jamison said just as firmly.

"Jamison, what's going on? Are you looking for something down here?" Sophie asked.

"I just need to take a quick look around and then I will leave," Jamison said.

Sophie recognized the shakiness and desperation in his voice. All his non-verbal cues were pointing to the fact that this was not a violent man, but a distressed and anxious man. He was unpredictable. She had to tread lightly so as not to back him into a corner and have him become violent.

"Just tell me what's going on. Is there something I can do to help?" Sophie asked, trying to calm her voice in the process.

The years of secrecy and frustration caught up with him in this moment and Sophie's empathetic tone was the lever that let the flood gates open.

"I know there may be something hidden down here. I don't know exactly what it is but if we work together, we can figure it out. Whatever we find, it's yours. If you need it that bad. But we need to find it first. If there is anything to find," Sophie said.

Jamison's shoulders sank like the weight of the world was about to be lifted. He reached into his pocket and pulled out a dark object and held it up to Sophie. Justin charged into the room, lunging at Jamison after seeing him holding something up toward Sophie and seeing the reddish-brown splatter on Sophie's white t-shirt.

"Wait!" Sophie yelled. "Stop!"

Jamison dropped the object on the floor as he jumped back out of Justin's reach.

Justin stopped just before he reached Jamison. He looked at Sophie with concern. "Are you okay" Pointing to her shirt.

Sophie completely forgot about the stain mishap. "Oh, yeah, I'm fine. Just a spill. I'm okay" she reassured him.

Justin eyed Jamison as if daring him to make a move. Sophie leaned down to pick up the object off the floor and saw it was a key. A unique skeleton key. Three loops on the end with a smaller loop in the middle. The key was worn looking with its years of scuffs and scratches on the gold covered exterior.

"I'm guessing you withheld this the other night when we were at your house?" Sophie said, holding up the key.

"What else have you not told her?" Justin asked with a scornful tone. "Were you even interested in a partnership, or did you just want access to the building?

"You have no idea what you're getting into. You should stay out of this, Justin," Jamison said in an irritated tone.

Sophie took charge of the situation, realizing it wasn't going anywhere productive. "Wait, let's all take a step back for a second. Jamison must have an important reason for being down here to go to all this trouble. Let's hear him out."

"How do we know he's even going to be straight with us?" Justin said. "He hid the key from you. He failed to mention that he was related to one of the original owners, and he withheld the name of the lady in the photograph. All things he must have known being an expert with this history as he claimed the other night. So why hide the identity of your grandmother?" Justin asked.

"Your grandmother? The woman in the photo?" Jamison asked, sounding genuinely surprised.

"Roselyn Mackenzie was my great-grandmother. We had just found that out when you ran into us in the diner the other day. We also found out that Hazel was her daughter. So, you can understand our skepticism," Sophie said.

Jamison took a few steps around the room, processing the

information. He pulled a high-back chair over to the two others surrounding a small, low table. He sat down in the chair hoping they would follow. Sophie followed right away. Justin was a bit more hesitant. Sophie looked up at Justin and then he took a seat next to her. They waited for Jamison to start.

"Macie Brooks was my grandmother. She suddenly left town and gave the responsibility of the business to Eddie Stone. He ran things for many years and then his wife's family took over. His son was in the military, so he was owner of record but didn't have time to run the day to day," Jamison said.

"Ezra Stone?" Sophie asked.

"Yes, that's right. When Macie left, she became emotionally distant to her son, my father. She was distracted and distant with her family and there were many rumors going around about her leaving due some sort of wedge between her and her partners. Rumors about some family secret. My father became consumed by this and saved photos, articles, journals, anything he could to try to find out the truth. His search led to dead ends. Then there was talk that something was hidden down here by one of the original three owners. I have no idea what it could be. I have heard it could be something worth monetary value or could be a clue leading to something else," Jamison said.

"So, you're looking for buried treasure or something?" Justin said still irritated.

"The phone call the other day at your house. Mae sounded bothered, maybe a little anxious. Does that have anything to do with this?" Sophie asked.

Jamison hesitated and looked down at the floor, debating whether or not to answer.

"Just want to get all the cards on the table," Sophie said.

"I'm guessing it does, given his silence," Justin added.

"The man on the phone believes that there is a buried treasure, as you called it." Looking at Justin. "He wants me to find it and is getting impatient," Jamison said, giving up on the attitude toward Justin. Exhausted by the years of stress and frustration.

"Is he threatening you?" Sophie asked.

"He has been withholding certificates and licenses that I need for some of the construction jobs I have been doing. It's making things very difficult for me. He has even stopped by the house a couple times when I wasn't home, harassing Mae. We don't know what he will do next. And I don't want to find out."

"So, he's a city official?" Justin asked with less of an attitude now.

"He's the City Manager," Sophie said. Justin and Jamison both looked at Sophie, surprised that she had that information. "I was there the other day dropping off paperwork. I saw him outside the building. I'm not positive but I think he was talking to one of the guys that broke in the other night. I wondered what the connection was. That makes sense now."

"Sending his thugs to do his dirty work," Justin said.

"Are there other contractors having the same issues that you know of?" Sophie asked, remembering witnessing the irate man in the hoodie with the construction company logo on it at the city office.

"Yes. There are a couple others that I have heard of having issues. Any that won't give him what he wants I suppose," Jamison said.

"So, let's get started," Sophie said, standing up.

The three of them spread out around the room, each of them dedicated to checking every crack and crevice in the room, hoping to find something that would help put to rest generations of questions. Sophie felt an unexplained energy and peace in the space, contrasting the moments after she first arrived in the room. Maybe it was the energy of the three of them on a mission. Maybe it was Hazel's spirit guiding her.

Either way, she was compelled to search behind the bar. She walked around the side of it, searching the area, looking for any obvious hiding places. She imagined herself with an object that she had to put away quickly. She thought about where she might consider safe places. She reached under the shelves. She searched the floor for loose or out of place boards.

"Any luck?" Jamison asked.

"Not just yet," Sophie said. She didn't know how, but she knew it was close.

She noticed how the walls were covered with old pictures in frames, always in groups. There was one lone picture hanging on the back wall. The frame was a little larger than all the others. Sophie carefully tilted the bottom of the picture to the left, exposing some loose brick.

"Think I found something," Sophie said.

CHAPTER 27

After clearing out the loose brick in the wall behind the picture frame, they found an opening the size of a small safe with enough space to hide cash, a weapon, or other sacred objects. The only item in the space was an envelope. Sophie removed the ivory envelope yellowed over the years and recognized the wax seal on the back. It was the same pattern as the one she recently bought at the antique market. She extended it out to Jamison to see if he wanted a closer look.

"Open it," he said, allowing her to do the honors.

She carefully broke open the wax seal and pulled several sheets of paper out of the envelope. She unfolded the papers revealing a handwritten letter signed by Eddie Stone. Sophie started reading the letter. "Looks like a confession. Or a confession of a confession, rather. The letter says that Macie went to Eddie and confided in him. She couldn't handle the guilt anymore after finding out that Hazel was found dead in the cellar storage room."

"Did she have something to do with it?" Jamison asked.

"Macie was angry about something that happened between the three of them and wanted revenge. It was no secret that Macie tended to be melodramatic. In a moment of rage, she went to the cellar storage room and destroyed the inventory of alcohol. She left and locked the door behind her. Hazel must have been hiding in the corner and Macie didn't see her. She had no idea the little girl followed her or came into the room at some point. Police thought Hazel did all the damage to the inventory from frantically trying to get out of the locked room. Apparently, she thinks Hazel fell and hit her head since the cause of death was trauma to her head," Sophie said.

"So, who did they think locked her in the room?" Justin asked.

"They must have never found out. Everything was based on rumors and speculation after that night. Nothing concrete," Jamison said.

"The letter says that Macie was going to stay silent about the whole thing and leave town. That she was afraid for her future. She couldn't face Roselyn and she was terrified that she would be blamed or even arrested. Roselyn blamed herself. She hesitated to call the police, worried that they would find the alcohol during the search. She feared fines or jail time. Never imagining this would be the outcome," Sophie said, studying and straightening the ivory pages after she finished reading the letter.

"The punishment she got was much worse than any that she could have dreaded," Jamison said.

"Her own mind was her enemy," Sophie said.

"What happened between the three of them that made Macie so angry in the first place?" Justin asked.

"It doesn't go into detail, but it ended up being some misunderstanding. Misinterpreting an overheard conversation," Sophie said.

"Speaking of misunderstandings, Jamison, I apologize for coming to the wrong conclusion when I came down here," Justin said.

"I'm the one that should be apologizing. I shouldn't have kept the information and the key from you. I thought that if I could just look around and find something, I could move past this. I could move on from all the years of wondering. All the years that my family has struggled not knowing the truth but suspecting something wasn't right," Jamison said.

"You could have just come to me and explained. We are partners," Sophie reminded him.

"I had no idea that your family was connected to this. I wanted to leave you out of it all," Jamison said.

"Was there ever any real interest in the business?" Sophie asked.

"Yes, of course. Even now I still have interest to continue. I think it could be a great thing. I think we could make something of it. But I understand if you don't want to continue with me as your partner. I know how important trust is. If I have ruined that for you, I understand and I truly am sorry," Jamison said.

"It may take some time for me to trust you again, but I am willing to try. This is uncharted water for me. It would be helpful to have a partner that I can count on. Plus, this is about more than just the two of us. People are counting on us to make this work. People, including Justin," Sophie said, motioning toward Justin. "I also want to honor Ezra's gift to me."

"I'm hoping we can put all this behind us. That someday you know that you can count on me. And we will always be connected through this chain of events," Jamison said.

"This chain of events has definitely affected all three families in different ways. Whatever the cause was doesn't matter right now. What matters is that at some point in time there was a connection that brought all of them together generations ago. Let's focus on that. Let's honor that. This building still has life," Sophie said.

"Then we need to finish what we started and restore this place," Jamison said.

"I think it could be even better than what it was," Sophie added.

"Ezra must have known what he was doing. Maybe he wanted to make sure the building got back to the right person," Justin said.

"There is one problem. I still have a city official to contend with. He's not going to be happy when he finds out the treasure he thought existed, turned out to be a letter of no use to him," Jamison said.

"You know what, leave the city manager to me. I have an idea," Sophie said.

"Be careful, Sophie. You don't know him. You don't want to make an enemy of him. This guy has more reach than you realize. He could make real problems for you. With this building, with your safety, or who knows what else he is capable of," Jamison warned her.

Sophie feared it was about more than just her now. Pacing back and forth around the room, she thought of Justin and Charlie. She thought of the problems the city manager could create for them. There could be severe consequences if she pursued any action against him. Afterall, Jamison knew firsthand how ruthless this man was. Then the answer became clear, as if someone whispered it in her ear. She stopped and stood still. That was absolutely right. It was about more than just her now. She was not alone and she had help. She refused to be a victim of her own mind. She paused for a few more seconds, a new plan revving its engine in her mind. "If he is connected to those men, he made an enemy of me the night he sent them. We have to do something. For all of us," Sophie said. Justin and Jamison nodded in agreement. "Alright then. Let's give him the unexpected."

CHAPTER 28

Sophie reached out to Max to enlist his help with her mission, which she called Operation Indigo. He suggested getting a friend of his from the police department involved. Max called back a short time later and informed her of the bad news that his contact with the police department fell through and wasn't going to be able to help, claiming it was a jurisdiction issue. Max got the impression it had to do with more of the city manager's reach. This complicated their efforts even more, raising Jamison's concerns. He was unsure if going through with it was the best option.

Sophie played out a few scenarios in her head. Trying to adjust for what she could but realizing that it was impossible to see through every detail. She was reminded recently that some things you don't see coming and you just have to adapt. Risk is inevitable. She had no choice but to rely on faith. Some adjustments had to be made from the original idea. Jamison was comfortable with the adjustments, especially him taking more of a backseat role. Three days later, the mission was set into motion.

Sophie had Max in mind for a different purpose. He was going to play the role of a contractor for the day. He had some background knowledge of construction, at least enough to get by. More importantly, he had the experience of persuasion in the courtroom to pull off the performance. Plus, just the right amount of arrogance, personality, and spirit of adventure. Justin was able to borrow a work van from his friend at the auto shop for the day. He was going to play the role of the driver. Harlan had a friend, Adam Garcia, that retired from the police department and was now a private investigator. He was excited to have the challenge and willing to help in any way he could. Adam was able to provide the surveillance equipment they needed.

The morning of Operation Indigo, the team agreed to meet at Jamison's house to go over the details and make any necessary last-minute adjustments. They got an early start and Mae had a breakfast buffet ready for them. Nerves were heightened with a mix of excitement and anxiousness. Mae offered to entertain Grayce and Charlie for the day, especially now that the little girl and Chili had become inseparable. As Harlan, Jamison, Justin, Max, and Adam sat out on the brick paved patio, the wooded area on the back edge of their property provided seclusion for their conversation. Sophie ran down the agenda for the day, including details on each person's task. Jamison knew the city manager's schedule and when he would be in his office. They all had their assignments and were ready to complete the mission.

The silver cargo van had plenty of space to house all of them. They arrived at city hall and parked in the municipal lot around ten o'clock in the morning to ensure the city manager was out of his meeting. Max stepped out of the van, dressed like he just rolled around in the middle of a renovation project. He wore white painter's pants with various color smudges, work boots that have seen a lot of miles, and a gently used T-shirt, complete with logo from a client of his that owns a construction company. Max made his way inside city hall to the building department counter.

A petite woman with a blond pixie cut and a raspy voice

greeted him at the counter. No smile, just a monotone voice. Short and to the point, as if being overly friendly was not in her job description. "Can I help you?" the woman asked.

"Hi. Rough day?" Max asked. "I hear it's statistically proven that if you smile at least once an hour, the day goes by faster." He continued, hoping for a positive reaction from the lady.

The lady smiled and immediately greeted him with a warmer tone. "What brings you in today?"

"See, it will be five o'clock before you know it," Max said.

The lady leaned in toward the counter and spoke in just above a whisper to avoid earshot of the man in the office a few feet away. "If you knew my boss, you'd understand," she said, nodding her head in the direction of his office.

Max nodded back and winked at her. Then he gauged how much louder he had to speak to gain the attention of the man in the office. "I need to change the name on a permit request. I'm the new contractor on the project."

"Alright and what is the address of the property or the name of the business it would be under?" the lady asked, typing on the keyboard of the computer.

"It's for the Blue Owl," Max said, raising his tone a little more, hoping to get a bite. He waited a few seconds, hoping the man would step out of his office. Nothing yet.

"Okay, can I have your name please?" the lady asked.

The city manager came out of his office with intention. "Actually, I can take care of this one. That way you can go to lunch," the city manager said with authority.

"He's all yours," she said, smiling at Max.

"Come on back to my office." He waved Max back and then turned toward his office.

Max whispered into his chest, attempting to entertain his audience. "Hook, line, and give me about five minutes for the sinker."

Max read the oversized gold name plate on the desk as the man ushered him into one of the hunter green velvet bucket chairs. "So, you're Sturgis H. Beel, I'm guessing?"

"Ahh, call me Stu," he said as he sat down and adjusted to get comfortable in his desk chair.

"Alright, Stu, I'm Max. What does the H stand for?"

"Herring, my father was a fisherman." He shrugged his shoulders. "So, Max, what can I do for you?"

"Well, I need to have the pending permits for a renovation project transferred into my name. The other contractor is no longer involved," Max said.

"And which project? I thought I heard you say the Blue Owl?"

"That's right," Max said.

"Absolutely, I can do that right now for you," Stu said, focusing on his computer screen.

"Great, and I also need to apply for a demolition permit. If it's not too much trouble."

"Quite a project going on there, it sounds like. What kind of demo work are you doing?"

"Removing an interior wall in the cellar. There is a lot of history to the place. The new owner may have found something behind the wall," Max said, trying to spark intrigue.

"Really? So, what happened with the previous contractor? You said he's not involved anymore?"

"No, can we keep this just between us?" Max asked leaning in.

"Sure. Sure. Absolutely," Stu said.

"The owner had good information that there was something of value hidden in the walls. She found out the location in an old letter connected to her family."

"Like a buried treasure?" Stu asked.

"Exactly like that," Max agreed. He leaned closer and lowered his voice slightly for effect. "She started to have suspicions of him. She caught him poking around the place a few times and just got a strange vibe. So, she wanted him out before that wall comes down," Max said.

"Did she confront him to see what he was doing?" Stu asked.

"Yeah, she sure did. She walked in one day, he was searching around behind pictures, checking floorboards, looking in drawers. He said he was just taking measurements for renovations, but she didn't believe him," Max said.

"Hmm. That is strange. Was there anyone else involved? Other treasure seekers?" Stu asked.

"Why? Do you think there was someone else behind it?" Max asked, already knowing the answer.

Stu, ignoring Max's question, said, "Hmm. You know, a hidden treasure could be of value to this city. Something newsworthy. In the right hands it could do a lot of good."

"Oh, I think this is newsworthy for sure," Max said, sitting back in the chair.

"You give me the impression that you are a smart guy. Would you be interested in a little side work? For the city?" Stu asked.

"What do you have in mind?" Max asked.

"Hypothetically speaking, let's say your demo permit is granted today. And let's say you tear down that wall. If there is something of value found, how would you feel about turning it over to your City Manager? For a finder's fee, of course," Stu said.

"How much of a finder's fee are we talking?" Max asked.

"Well, I guess that depends on a couple of things," Stu said.

"And what things are those?"

"How fast you are able to get the demo done, what you find, if indeed you find anything, and if you are able to keep quiet about it," Stu said.

"Hypothetically speaking again, Stu. If I were to say yes to bringing you this mysterious hidden treasure buried in the walls of the Blue Owl, would I have any issues with future permits?" Max asked.

"I'm sure we can accommodate you," Stu said.

"So, what happens if I do find something, and it's given to the owner?" Max asked.

"As I said, you seem like a smart guy. That could be devastating to any future business. You know, permits, licenses, inspections, you get the idea. Paperwork gets lost around here all the time," Stu said.

"I'm definitely getting the idea," Max said, nodding his head.

"Great! So, we understand each other?" Stu asked.

"Absolutely."

"Alright. I'm glad you're on board. Just need some information from you and then you can be on your way. What's your last name, Max?"

Max looked around the office with outdated green and brown décor. He noticed a framed picture of a golf course on the wall. "Green. It's Max Green."

Stu typing on his computer, entering the information. "And the name of the company?"

Max continued looking around the room, completely forgetting about the company logo on the breast area of his shirt. His eyes paused on a gaudy lamp resting on the credenza to his left. He caught Stu's gaze after the pause. "Lighthouse Renovations LLC." Realizing after he gave the name that the logo and the name he just offered did not match, he casually rested his elbow on the chair and lifted his wrist up to cover the logo. He hoped Stu was not quick enough to notice. Although there were a tense few seconds, Max would not let a logo on a T-shirt lead to the operation's demise.

While Stu was entering the information on his computer, Max slid in one last question. "Oh, just out of curiosity, are there any others out there helping you find these valuable items that I should be aware of?"

"None you need to be aware of. I had a few others, but they couldn't get the job done." Stu's eyes shifted sternly from his computer screen to Max's eyes. "You're all set. I'm done here." Stu printed a copy of the permit and handed it to Max.

"Yeah, I think you are," Max said under his breath as he stood up and turned his head toward the exit.

"What's that?" Stu asked.

"That's a nice car." Max pointed to the picture of an orange 1973 Pantera complete with a spoiler on the back.

Stu stood up, adjusting his pants around his stout body and rested his hands on his hips.

"Yep, a fine Italian automobile." He started walking toward the door to walk Max out.

Max, wanting to avoid a lengthy conversation about a car that was clearly more Stu's style than his, was first to end the meeting. "Great, thanks. I think I got everything I need," he said as he stepped through the office doorway.

"So, who's Busted?" Stu asked.

Max whirled around, wide-eyed. "Pardon?" he forced himself to ask as casually as possible. Hoping he did not just hear his voice crack slightly.

"Busted. Demo and Concrete," Stu said, reading it off the logo on Max's shirt. "Is that you?"

"Guilty as charged."

"I thought it was Lighthouse Renovations." Stu said.

Max was now in lawyer mode, thoroughly irritated that this overconfident, suited criminal was acting like he had something on Max and was going to trip him up. "It can't possibly be the first time, in your line of work, that you have encountered someone with multiple businesses. Is it?"

"See you soon," Stu said.

Max walked out of City Hall and back to the van with everything they needed to get the authorities involved and bring charges against Sturgis H. Beel.

CHAPTER 29

1929

MACIE

Two tall windows covered in heavy burgundy, ceiling-to-floor drapes, were cracked open slightly in an effort to let the winter air breathe into the small studio apartment. The air was still, as was the street below. A small round dining table held a half-drank bottle of whiskey and the highball glass next to it, now empty, held a fresh dark red lipstick stain on it. The large floor length mirror in the corner of the bedroom area held a reflection. A tired and worn face. Too worn for her late youth. Slightly dried tears mixed with mascara and rouge ran down the length of her cheeks.

Macie, lost in the reflection in the mirror, barely recognized herself. She was disturbed by how drastically her life had changed in such a brief time. The devastating news regarding Hazel's death came earlier that day. A momentary numbness from the whiskey kicked in but she knew it would only temporarily mask the anguish.

The timeline of that dreadful night replayed in her head.

She was convinced she had to be the last one in that cellar. Otherwise, the destruction in the storage room would have been noticed prior to the tragic event. Macie retraced her steps. She remembered locking the storage room door behind her. The authorities claimed the theory that Hazel, while in a panicked frenzy, was responsible for damages to the room and its contents. Macie knew better. What she did not know was how Hazel occupied the room unnoticed. She did not remember seeing anyone in the cellar and Hazel was sitting cozily in the office chair that night when she left her.

Macie closed her eyes in attempt to visualize the evening in her mind more clearly. Was there something she missed? The lion. The stuffed lion laying on the ground just inside the cellar storage room doorway. It was in the shadow, but she saw it. The same lion was held by the little girl moments before, in the office. Macie could picture Hazel waving to her with the small lion's paw.

At that moment, Macie realized the significance of her role in the tragedy. There was no going back. She opened her eyes and stared at her reflection again, trying to wipe the black streaks off her face. The stubborn stains clung to her skin, she rubbed harder and harder until it smudged even more around her face. Emotion came to a head, and she fell to her knees sobbing into the floorboards. The wood, cool against her cheeks.

The make-up mess on her face was insignificant compared to the mess her life was now. What were the options? Go to the police and let them know what happened. There was no way they would believe her. What if she became a murder suspect? Go tell Roselyn what happened. Tell her the truth, that she was angry and hurt and took revenge on the inventory out of frustration. That option may lead back to the police as well. Out of self-preservation, she had to avoid anything that would incriminate her.

She could not confront Roselyn either. The guilt and thought of seeing Roselyn's face was overwhelming. Roselyn would never forgive her. Macie could never forgive herself, so how would Roselyn be able to get past it? She believed they did not want her there anyway which is what started the whole thing. That had to be it. Macie was having trouble focusing on what led her down the path of destruction in the first place. What was it really? An assumption? A misunderstanding? Was it as bad as she thought? It was too late now. Too late for understanding. Too late for reconciliation. Especially now, with collateral damage. Macie could not face that. She had to leave town. She was convinced that was her only option. She may not have killed Hazel, but she did not feel innocent in the outcome. She had to leave, now. She could not face Roselyn, at least not yet. She needed time to figure things out.

Macie paced at first, the small wood planks of her second story apartment creaking beneath her feet. The apartment was small but all she required. She went over to the closet door and turned the crystal knob. She pulled out her two-tone brown, hard-shell suitcase, tossed it on top of the rose-colored chenille bedspread and flipped open the latches. Moving back and forth from the dresser to the nightstand, she grabbed clothing and other items. She stuffed her belongings randomly into the suitcase. She pulled the rainy-day cash out from under the mattress and shoved it inside the suitcase pocket. Macie wanted to leave first thing in the morning. She had one last stop to make. One thing to do before leaving town. She had to see Eddie. Tonight. One last time. She had to tell him what happened. Even after everything, she felt she could trust Eddie. She wanted at least one person to know her side of the story.

CHAPTER 30

PRESENT DAY

A thin, powdery coat of drywall dust settled on any available flat surface along with boxes of screws, nails, new light fixtures, and other evidence that renovations were in full swing. There was excitement from the commotion of contractors moving about with their tool chests, small lunchbox coolers, water bottles, and various fountain drink cups scattered around. The smell of fresh paint filled the air, bringing in a sense of newness.

Jamison ended his phone call with a huff. Sophie walked between the crew of workers installing light fixtures over to the side of the room where he was standing and starting to pace.

Scratching his head, Jamison said, "We're not going to make it."

"What's wrong?" Sophie asked.

Jamison set his pen and clipboard down on a brand-new light fixture box. "I don't see how we are going to finish in time for the grand opening. I just got off the phone with the granite company. There was a mix up with our granite for the restroom vanities."

"Alright, it can't be that bad. Is it?" Sophie asked.

"Apparently, the warehouse sent our slab to the wrong fabricator. They cut it and when they went to install it, not only did the customer notice it was the wrong piece of granite but that it was cracked. When our fabricator requested another slab, the warehouse claims it was the last one in that style." Jamison paused, thinking of all the items in the timeline that would be thrown off by the setbacks. "It gets better. Also, city inspections are backed up because of the complications with the city manager investigation. Everything is at a standstill," Jamison said, running his hands through his hair and resting them on his head to cope with the stress of the moment.

Sophie paused and glanced around at all the disarray of the building. This was something that would have bothered her a couple month ago. She was pleased with all the progress that had been made over the past several weeks and she intended to see it through. "Well, let's take this one obstacle at a time. It's going to happen. We just need to figure out how. Easy right?" Sophie shrugged her shoulders and gave Jamison a supportive smile.

"I think we are going to have to push back the opening," Jamison repeated.

"Here is what we are going to do: call the warehouse and see if they have a slab that is similar to what we chose. Have them put a rush on getting it to the fabricator so they can install it as soon as they can. If they don't have anything close, there has to be another warehouse around with something in their stock that will work. Anything similar to what we picked will be fine. As far as the inspections, let it play out for a bit before we get too concerned. Give it a couple more days. We will figure something out," Sophie said.

Charlie announced the arrival of the delivery truck, hopped off her lookout spot near the window and bounced over to Sophie.

"I will call them back right now," Jamison said, pulling out his phone as he headed outside to oversee the delivery.

"Great! I'm going to focus on hiring a chef. Charlie, do you want to come help with an important decision of the day?"

"Yes," the little girl said firmly, proud to be of assistance. Sophie took her petite hand and led her through the kitchen door and propped her up on the stainless-steel countertop.

The chef she was considering was whipping up some tasty samples of macaroni and cheese, pulled pork, and salmon with mango glaze. While Charlie was testing the macaroni and cheese, Sophie put some of the small sample cups on a tray and took them to the workers. She wanted to get the consensus to see if he was Blue Owl material.

Jamison ran into Grayce out in front of the building while he was carrying the last load of liquor bottles from the delivery truck. She wanted to see the progress made on the building renovations since her last visit, but more importantly, she had a more informative visit in mind.

"Grayce!" Sophie was pleasantly surprised to see her as she entered the doorway, right behind Jamison. "Welcome to our construction zone," Sophie said, motioning to all the chaos going on around them.

"Hello love! Just the person I wanted to see." They embraced in a friendly hug, demonstrating the familiarity that existed since their first introduction. "Wow, this is really going to be something when it's finished. I can see the transformation already," Grayce said, looking around the room.

"That is, if we can get past these roadblocks," Jamison said, coming over to join them after setting the box down on the bar.

Grayce looked at Sophie with concern, seeking more clarification. "The biggest issue is, they have stopped all inspections due to the city manager investigation. Apparently, it is a mess over there. If we don't get our inspection done in time, we don't get the all-clear to open," Sophie said.

"That's what I stopped by to talk to you about. I heard that Mr. Beel is NOT going to face prosecution," Grayce said.

"Why not? What happened?" Sophie asked.

"Either the influence he has or a lack of evidence against him," Grayce said.

"Or just his elusive nature," Jamison added, shaking his head with dissatisfaction.

"However, they did ask him to resign his position as city manager," Grayce said.

"So basically, a slap on the wrist," Sophie added.

"Exactly," Grayce continued. "That's why it is a mess over there. They found several other issues that he had caused. They are sorting out what they can."

"How did you find this out?" Sophie asked.

"I have a friend in the building department. If it's an inspection you need, I can make a phone call," Grayce said, willing to accommodate anything they needed.

"That would be great! We would really appreciate the help," Sophie said.

"And, what if Mr. Beel decides to make an appearance here?" Jamison asked, dissatisfaction turning to worry.

"Then we'll be ready for him," Sophie said.

"I don't think that will be necessary. He is—or maybe has already—left the area. It's in his best interest not to stick around, so he shouldn't bother you. Plus, I don't think he made a connection between any of you and the day Max was in his office," Grayce said, trying to reassure them.

"Well, I guess that's somewhat of a relief then," Sophie said.

The chef patiently waiting in the kitchen peeked his head out the door to locate Sophie. There was a smaller head peeking out a few feet below his.

"I think you are being summoned," Jamison said to Sophie, motioning toward the kitchen door. "By the chef and his assistant."

"Oh, that's right! He's been waiting for me to come back in there. I hope number four is a winner," Sophie said with a smile.

"Number four?" Grayce asked.

"Number one and two weren't what I was looking for and number three was a no show. But I think number four is the one. What did you think of the samples?"

"I think we found our chef," Jamison said.

Justin came out of the kitchen wiping his hands on the white apron tied around his waist. He walked over to join the group. Charlie followed close behind with a couple more food samples for Grayce. Sophie congratulated Justin on earning his new chef status.

"It's going to be a wonderful gathering space with excellent food it sounds like," Grayce said. "With all these changes, are you going to keep the Blue Owl Bar name?"

"Yes, I would like to honor tradition, but I'm not stuck on Bar. Something about it doesn't settle. I want to give it our own flair too," Sophie said.

"You know, it reminds me of this cozy tavern Harlan and I went to years ago," Grayce said, and the Blue Owl Tavern was born.

CHAPTER 31

The night of the grand opening of the Blue Owl Tavern finally arrived. All the renovations were complete, and it was ready to see its first customers in several years. Some of the original features were restored with its old-style charm. Updated light fixtures and furniture pieces added a twist to welcome the Blue Owl into the modern day. They even restored the original style of the speakeasy down in the lower level in the Indigo Room. Overall, there was a thick wood and leather atmosphere with cozy, inviting lighting. The liquor cabinet was fully stocked. The glasses were sparkling and the ice bins were full. The kitchen was fully functioning with new appliances. In just a few hours they would open their doors.

Sophie was in the kitchen leaning over the new, shiny stainless counter, inserting the candles into the cakes. Eight for Charlie's birthday in the round cake and one in the blue, owl shaped cake. Justin entered the kitchen and walked up behind Sophie, wrapping his arms around her waist.

"Can I help with anything?"

"I'll be happy to answer that later." She leaned up and kissed him. "But for now, just the door."

"My pleasure." Justin smiled. "Tonight's going to be great. Looks amazing. You ready?"

"Bring on OUR next adventure," Sophie said.

Justin looked out into the room full of people as he pushed open the swinging door. "Let's give 'em the ol' razzle-dazzle!"

Sophie carried the tray with both cakes into the main area. Two long tables were set up with groups of light pink, fuchsia, navy, and turquoise balloons at each end. They were covered with white tablecloths and clear, square vases in the center holding fresh-cut pink roses with coordinating accent flowers. As she walked up to the table and set the tray of cakes down in the center, Sophie admired the abundance of people gathered for Charlie's birthday. They were all like family to her, even after a few months. Marcella and Sam were seated next to Charlie, in the middle of the table. Max standing behind them, glass in hand, was chatting with Justin, Jamison, and Adam. Mae, seated on the other side of Charlie, was fixing the untied bow on the back of Charlie's bright pink dress, her favorite color. Harlan and Grayce were walking back from the serving area bringing drink refills.

"Cake time!" Marcella shouted in an attempt to gather everyone around while Sophie lit the candles on both cakes.

Harlan led the group in singing Happy Birthday. Charlie made a wish and eagerly blew out the candles. After the cheers finished, Justin quietly asked Charlie if she wanted to say anything to the group.

"Thank you everyone for celebrating my birthday and for the presents," Charlie said as the group responded with more cheers.

"We definitely have a lot to celebrate tonight," Sophie said.

"Speech! Speech!" Harlan added as the others chimed in.

Sophie holding up her glass, "To Ezra, for giving me an opportunity I didn't even know existed. To Roselyn, Eddie, and Macie, I hope we can honor what they started generations ago. To Hazel, guiding us to find the key to the past." Holding her glass higher. "And to all of you, being here to celebrate."

They all held up their glasses and drank while the music

played in the background.

Sophie regarded the décor and the architecture with a sense of peace and satisfaction. All the hours put in to making this once run-down, vacant piece of real estate with a future of uncertainty into something restored that had a chance to be stronger with new generations. Putting to rest secrets of generations past and creating second chances, forgiveness, and hope for newly strengthened relationships. She was thankful for the opportunity, something she could be a part of. She thought about how different her life might have been if she had not taken the detour on an unexpected and unfamiliar road. What if she had continued down the original path that she created for some time, ignoring her true voice? She reflected on the people that she met along the way, finding a lost connection to family that she had been longing for. There was a peaceful energy flowing through the building that was once filled with darkness.

The grand opening of the Blue Owl Tavern was in full swing. Patrons came in at a steady pace. Drinks were flowing, the grill was sizzling, and jukebox music added a nice ambiance to the experience of the guests enjoying each other's company. Sophie was making rounds, socializing with the guests, making sure their experience was satisfactory. Marcella was in her glory, making specialty mixed drinks and entertaining the constant flow of people occupying the seats.

Justin held the door open for a woman in her late fifties. A long, flowing skirt swept from side to side as she approached the end of the bar and sat down. Her bright-colored, patterned tunic top stood out against her dark skin. The large tribal styled necklace and bracelet were visible from across the room. Marcella noticed her right away and made her way over to take the woman's drink order.

"Welcome to the Blue Owl. What can I make for you?" Marcella asked the woman, wearing a warm smile. Her short black hair with tight to the head waves revealed her well-balanced features, high cheekbones, and large, gold dangling earrings.

"I'm looking for Sophie," the woman said in a pleasant inquiring tone.

"Sure, let me find her and I will send her right over," Marcella said, accommodating her request.

Sophie approached the woman and sat on the stool next to her. "Hello. I'm Sophie. I hear you were looking for me."

"Yes, hello. I wanted to inquire about renting the space next door," the woman said.

"Oh." Sophie paused, sounding a little surprised. "Yes. I am thinking about renting it, but I haven't advertised yet. Where did you hear about it?" Sophie asked.

"Oh, here and there," the woman responded vaguely.

"When are you wanting to rent?" Sophie asked.

"Right away. I'm ready as soon as it's available. I just moved up here from New Orleans. I'm looking for space for my store."

"Sounds great. I can give you a call tomorrow and we can go over the details. Stay and enjoy a meal on the house," Sophie offered.

"I wish I could. But I must be going," the woman said as she stood up from the stool to leave.

"What's your name?" Sophie asked.

"I'm Eve." She reached out to shake Sophie's hand.

Sophie extended her hand to the woman. Eve gently grasped ahold and put her other hand on top of Sophie's. Her grip lingering softly. Sophie looked down at her hand and then into the woman's large dark brown eyes. Sophie got the impression that this woman knew something that everyone else in the room didn't. With heavy eyes, her gaze looked as though she were staring into Sophie's soul.

"Do you have a number where I can reach you?" Sophie

asked, breaking away.

"I'll find you," Eve replied and smiled kindly.

"Okay, until tomorrow then," Sophie added.

The woman took a couple steps, starting toward the door. She stopped and turned back toward Sophie. "Roselyn says thank you."

ACKNOWLEDGMENTS

Thank you to my husband for the engaging conversations, continually and graciously listening to me bounce off ideas, my daughter for always being my biggest cheerleader, and my son, for accountability, asking "did you finish your book yet?" Thank you to my mom for being my first proofreader and boost of moral support.

I also want to thank Tami Ford, Celia Mulder, Maria Graessle, Alison Voakes, Meredith Voakes, Corey LaValley and Dr. Rachal Mittleman for your interest, support, and helpful feedback. Shout out to Kristi from the block and Aunt Ester for agreeing to read early drafts.

I am grateful for the team of welcoming, knowledgeable, great human beings at Atmosphere Press. I appreciate your experience, expertise, and guidance on my publishing journey.

Thank you to all the readers out there who dare to open the cover.

ABOUT ATMOSPHERE PRESS

Atmosphere Press is an independent, full-service publisher for excellent books in all genres and for all audiences. Learn more about what we do at atmospherepress.com.

We encourage you to check out some of Atmosphere's latest releases, which are available at Amazon.com and via order from your local bookstore:

Icarus Never Flew 'Round Here, by Matt Edwards

COMFREY, WYOMING: Maiden Voyage, by Daphne Birkmeyer

The Chimera Wolf, by P.A. Power

Umbilical, by Jane Kay

The Two-Blood Lion, by Nick Westfield

Shogun of the Heavens: The Fall of Immortals, by I.D.G. Curry

Hot Air Rising, by Matthew Taylor

30 Summers, by A.S. Randall

Delilah Recovered, by Amelia Estelle Dellos

A Prophecy in Ash, by Julie Zantopoulos

The Killer Half, by JB Blake

Ocean Lessons, by Karen Lethlean

Unrealized Fantasies, by Marilyn Whitehorse

The Mayari Chronicles: Initium, by Karen McClain

Squeeze Plays, by Jeffrey Marshall

JADA: Just Another Dead Animal, by James Morris

Hart Street and Main: Metamorphosis, by Tabitha Sprunger

Karma One, by Colleen Hollis

Ndalla's World, by Beth Franz

Adonai, by Arman Isayan

The Journey, by Khozem Poonawala

Stolen Lives, by Dee Arianne Rockwood

ABOUT THE AUTHOR

Winegarden Photography

Hidden Shadow is Jennifer's first novel. She is a wife, mother, and entrepreneur with a graduate degree from Marygrove College and a bachelor's degree from Central Michigan University. Jennifer believes in the importance of kindness and the healing power of dogs, humor, and writing. She appreciates creativity, palm trees and a good margarita.

Made in the USA
Columbia, SC
26 November 2022